GIFT OF

John Warren Stewig

Carthage

Lizzie Silver of Sherwood Forest

Also by Marilyn Singer

It Can't Hurt Forever
Tarantulas on the Brain
(the first book about Lizzie Silver)

THE SAM AND DAVE MYSTERIES
The Case of the Cackling Car
The Case of the Sabotaged School Play
A Clue in Code
Leroy Is Missing

FOR YOUNG ADULTS
The Course of True Love Never Did Run Smooth
The First Few Friends

Lizzie Silver
of Sherwood
Forest

by Marilyn Singer

illustrated by
Miriam Nerlove

1   8      1   7

HARPER & ROW, PUBLISHERS

Cambridge, Philadelphia, San Francisco, London, Mexico City, São Paolo, Singapore, Sydney

NEW YORK

Special thanks to Steve Aronson and Dulcie Barlow

Lizzie Silver of Sherwood Forest
Text copyright © 1986 by Marilyn Singer
Illustrations copyright © 1986 by Miriam Nerlove
All rights reserved. No part of this book may be
used or reproduced in any manner whatsoever without
written permission except in the case of brief quotations
embodied in critical articles and reviews. Printed in
the United States of America. For information address
Harper & Row Junior Books, 10 East 53rd Street,
New York, N.Y. 10022. Published simultaneously in
Canada by Fitzhenry & Whiteside Limited, Toronto.
Designed by Joyce Hopkins
1 2 3 4 5 6 7 8 9 10
First Edition

Library of Congress Cataloging-in-Publication Data
Singer, Marilyn.
   Lizzie Silver of Sherwood Forest.

   Summary: Inspired by the example of her latest
obsession, Robin Hood, Lizzie begins to scheme to
follow her best friend, Tessa, into music school.
   [1. Friendship—Fiction.   2. Robin Hood—Fiction]
I. Nerlove, Miriam, ill.   II. Title.
PZ7.S6172Li 1986   [Fic]   85-45263
ISBN 0-06-025621-4
ISBN 0-06-025622-2 (lib. bdg.)

To all of Lizzie's fans

Lizzie Silver
of Sherwood
Forest

1

"Take that! And that! And that!" I said. My sword rang
out against the Sheriff of Nottingham's. He was a good
swordsman. Too good. I couldn't hold him off much
longer. Suddenly, with a quick parry, he knocked my
sword out of my hands. He laughed a nasty laugh.
"Breathe your last, Maid Lizzie," he said, pressing the
sharp point of his sword against my throat.

Suddenly a flash of Lincoln green. "First you will
reckon with me, sir," said a low voice.

The Sheriff of Nottingham spun around. He was
face to face with Robin Hood. "Here, Elizabeth, catch!"
Robin called, tossing me my sword, just as three of the
sheriff's men found us. "Back to back!" ordered Robin.

I smiled. It was our favorite strategy. "Take that!" I
yelled, striking out. One of the sheriff's men fell. Robin

1

struck down another. We were evenly matched again.

And then Robin stumbled.

Out of the corner of my eye, I saw the sheriff raise his sword to deliver a deadly blow. I whirled around to fend it off . . .

"What are you doing in that weird position, Lizzie? Studying some new form of yoga?" my sister, Rona, said.

I dropped my arms and sat down on my bed. "How many times have I told you not to come into my room without knocking?"

Rona ignored my question. "I bet you were pretending to be Robin Hood again."

"I don't pretend to be Robin Hood," I said. "Robin Hood is a man."

"Robin Hood is a make-believe character, like Snow White or E.T.," said Rona.

"That's not true!" I yelled.

We'd had this argument before, Rona and me, and I always got angry at her during it. I don't know why I couldn't just ignore her. But I couldn't. I loved Robin Hood too much.

I found out about Robin Hood from Buster. Buster is my best friend Tessa's uncle. She doesn't like him that much, but I do. He used to dress up as famous Busters, like Buster Keaton and Buster Brown. He said it was to "wake people up," to surprise them. He doesn't do that anymore, though; he says a person shouldn't

2

always stick to the same thing to wake people up—and besides, he ran out of Busters. Anyway, Buster gave me this book called *Robin Hood of Sherwood Forest*. I don't much like books, but I sure liked that one. I read it so fast, Buster promised to get me another book with more stories about Robin Hood. I can't wait.

Mom says that Robin Hood is my latest *obsession*. I asked her what an obsession is, and she said it means when you never stop thinking of something or someone. She said Ariadne was my last obsession. Ariadne is my pet tarantula. I wanted a tarantula for a long time. I guess I did think about her a lot. And I did all sorts of things to get her. It was Buster who helped me in the end. But I didn't think about Ariadne *all* the time. I don't think about Robin Hood all the time either. I don't think about him when I sleep (except if I have a dream about him) or when I watch Ariadne (except sometimes).

Robin Hood is so great, living in Sherwood Forest with his band of Merry Men, tricking nasty, greedy people and helping poor ones. I don't like the fact that he shot a lot of animals, but that's how people got to eat in those days, I guess, so I'll forgive him for that. And I do like bows and arrows. I asked Mom if I could have an archery set for my birthday—a real set, not the kind with the suction cups instead of arrowheads—but she said, "I don't believe in buying my children weapons."

3

"He is made-up," Rona was still arguing. "Robin Hood is a fake!"

"He is not!" I yelled again. "You don't know anything. Buster says he was a real person." I got up, went over to Ariadne's cage and took off the top. I opened a jar and started dropping crickets from it into the cage. If there was one way to get Rona out of my room, that was it.

"Ugh!" she squealed, hiding her eyes. "Disgusting. That's disgusting! That creepy thing is always eating."

"She only eats once a week, and you know it. And if you don't by now, you've got even more empty space between your ears than I thought," I said.

"All right, Lizzie. That does it. For being so nasty, I'm not going to give you the message I've got for you." She turned to go.

I stopped feeding Ariadne. Uh-oh. A message. I thought fast. "You were nasty first," I said. "And if you don't tell me, I won't tell you what I overheard Toby Glickstein saying about you at the pool this morning."

Rona froze. She loved Toby Glickstein almost as much as I loved Robin Hood. "What did he say?"

"You give me my message first."

She scrunched up her mouth the way she does when she's making a tough decision. "All right," she finally said. "The message is that Tessa called and said she wants you to come right over before she goes to see

4

her grandmother. She said it's important."

I didn't say anything, but I got a tight feeling inside. Tessa's been my best friend for a while. She understands all about my obsessions and she doesn't make fun of them. Tessa never says something's important unless it really is. The only thing I could think of that was important enough for Tessa to call important was whether or not she got into Pemborough Music Conservatory. Pemborough is in upstate New York, so if Tessa got in, she'd go live there. And that was the last thing in the world I wanted to happen.

"Now," Rona said, interrupting my thoughts, "what did Toby Glickstein say?"

I shook my head a little to clear it and looked at Rona. She was trying not to seem too eager, but her fingers were twitching and she was tapping her foot.

"He said you have . . ." I paused dramatically.

She wet her lips. "What? What do I have?"

"Great teeth."

"What?" She looked like she'd just opened a fortune cookie and found there was nothing inside it. "That's all?"

"Yep. That's all."

"That's all he said? That I have great teeth? What does he think I am, a horse or something?"

"You look at a horse's teeth to tell how old it is. Toby already knows your age."

"Oh, shut up, Lizzie. Just shut up. I shouldn't have

come in here at all. That's what I get for being nice."
She marched out, slamming the door.

I shrugged and began to wonder what Robin Hood's
teeth were like. I bet they were straighter and whiter
than Rona's from chomping on all those legs of venison
he ate. And he sure never had to wear braces for five
years either. Lucky Robin. No braces and no sister like
Rona either. And lots of friends who stuck by his side
and didn't think about going to music school in some
other town.

I sighed and walked over to Ariadne's cage. I dropped
in two more crickets. And, softly, I began to sing:

> "Robin Hood, Robin Hood,
> Riding through the glen.
> Robin Hood, Robin Hood,
> With his band of men.
> Feared by the bad,
> Loved by the good,
> Robin Hood, Robin Hood, Robin Hood."

I sighed again and sang the song three more times
straight through until Ariadne had finished her last
cricket.

Then I picked myself up and said, "Let us ride,
Robin, and see what news the fair Lady Tessa has for
us."

"Lead on, Elizabeth," said Robin. "Lead on."
We steered our horses out the door.

2

Tessa looked weird. Her cheeks were too pink and her eyes too shiny. The bad feeling inside me got worse. But I tried to ignore it.

"Hi, Tessa, guess what? My dad taught me this great song about Robin Hood last night. He said . . ."

"Lizzie, I did it," Tessa interrupted quietly.

"It comes from an old TV show he watched when he was a kid. I wish they'd put it back on. . . ."

"I said I did it," she repeated.

"What did you do?" I asked, even though I knew what was coming.

"I got accepted to Pemborough."

I swallowed. "Oh," I said. "That's nice."

Tessa looked at me with frustration. "Is that all you're going to say?"

I swallowed again. There was a lot I wanted to say, but I didn't want to make Tessa even more frustrated. "I'm . . . uh . . . glad you . . . uh . . . got accepted . . ." I choked out.

Tessa kept staring at me. "School starts in two and a half months. The letter said I gave a fine audition and—"

I couldn't hold it in any longer. "Oh, Tessa," I wailed. "Don't go! I don't want you to go. You're my best friend!" I flung my arms around her.

She hugged me and sighed. "Oh, Lizzie. I don't want to go. I'll miss you too. You know I will."

"Then don't go," I blubbered. I was crying, and embarrassed because I was. I couldn't stand the thought of Tessa leaving. A month ago she had told me that her parents wanted her to go to Pemborough, and I'd asked her if there was a good place she could study piano in Brooklyn or Manhattan. "Not as good as Pemborough," she'd said. I got the chills thinking about her leaving. So I tried not to think about it. I did pretty well, too, except when the audition came up. And now.

"You told me you didn't want to hang around with a bunch of snotty music students. You said you didn't like that town Pemborough is in. You said—"

"Oh, Lizzie." Tessa sighed again. "I know I said those things. But my parents think I'll get a much better education there than if I go to a regular

junior high school in Brooklyn."

"But your parents aren't creeps," I said, trying to stop crying. "If you tell them you don't want to go, they won't make you."

"I know," Tessa answered quietly. "But I want to go."

"You just said you didn't."

"I do and I don't. Lizzie, I'm all confused." She sat down with her head in her hands.

I felt strange. Tessa was almost never confused. Not like me.

"Maybe you could wait until next year," I said.

Tessa looked up. "Why should I do that?"

"Then I could go, too."

"Huh? How could you go? You don't play the piano, or any other instrument either. You're not even interested in music. You're interested in science."

"I *am so* interested in music. I listen to the radio. And as for an instrument, I could learn."

"Lizzie . . ."

"I'll study something easy. Like—like the drums! I bet I could learn to play the drums."

"The drums aren't easy."

"Then I'll learn something else."

"What? The toy xylophone? Forget it, Lizzie."

"No, I won't. I bet you I can learn to play something well enough to get into Pemborough."

"Come on, Lizzie. It won't work. I have to let them

10

know by the middle of next month whether or not I'm coming."

"Can you tell whether or not somebody has musical talent?" I asked suddenly.

"No, but my piano teacher can."

I took a deep breath. "Okay, I bet you that by the middle of next month I can learn to play something well enough to show your piano teacher I have musical talent."

"So?" asked Tessa, puzzled.

"So if she says I do, in a year I'll be good enough to get into Pemborough."

"Hold it, Lizzie. Even if you have talent, you probably wouldn't get into Pemborough. You have to study for a long time to give a good audition."

"Would your teacher be able to tell after six weeks whether or not I could get in?"

"I don't think so."

"But there's a chance, right?"

"About one in a million."

"Good. That's still a chance. Then give me six weeks."

"Lizzy, you're crazy!"

"Six weeks. Promise you won't tell them yes until the six weeks are up."

Tessa sighed once more. "Okay. I promise."

I stuck out my pinky. Tessa linked it with hers.

Then Tessa said, "I've got to go visit my grandmother now."

"How's her ankle?" I asked. Grandma Brown had broken her ankle a few days before.

"Better. . . . See you later, Lizzie."

I nodded and left, wondering what Robin Hood would do now?

3

I raced home from Tessa's and up to my room. I knew I had to get started right away. I pulled out a big sheet of paper. At the top of it, I wrote: BECOMING A MUSICIAN PLAN. Beneath that, just the way Tessa'd taught me when I was trying to get Ariadne, I wrote:

Step   Problem   Solution.

Underneath *Step* I wrote A; and below *Problem* I put, "To Play an Instrument." I stared at it a minute and then erased it. It didn't seem right. It was what Tessa would call too general. She told me last time that you have to break the problem down to solve it. Let's see, I said to myself, I need to play an instrument well enough so that Tessa's teacher will say I've got talent and can get into Pemborough. In order to play an instrument, I have to learn how to. In order to learn how to, I have to take lessons. That's it! Lessons!

I was about to write that down when I realized there was still a step before taking lessons. And that was figuring out what instrument to take lessons in. I thought about that a minute, and then, satisfied it was Step A, I wrote it down like this:

Step	Problem
A	Finding out what instrument to play

So far, so good. Then I looked at the third column of my chart, *Solution.* And I frowned.

What instrument *do* I want to learn? I asked myself. I tried to think about the instruments I've heard. Guitar. Drums. Piano. Once, when I was in third grade, my teacher took us to a concert in a big hall. A whole orchestra performed. I closed my eyes and tried to picture the instruments, but I couldn't see anything besides some violins.

I needed help, but Buster was out of town and I couldn't call Tessa—not for this one. I had to solve it by myself. Then I thought, maybe I could try thinking the way Tessa does. "Now, Lizzie," I said aloud, imitating Tessa's voice, "you must get organized."

"I *am* organized," I said, in my own voice. "Look at this chart."

"Very impressive," I said in Tessa's voice. "So what's your problem?"

14

"My problem is I have to figure out what instrument to play, and I hardly know what any instruments sound like."

"Then you need to do some research."

"Tessa, you're a genius!" I said to myself, and I started to laugh, half because it was funny, but half because it had worked—I *had* thought like Tessa. And "Tessa" had come up with the right answer.

Research. I needed to do research. And that meant I had to go to the library.

I got up from the floor, picked up my backpack and ran downstairs and out the door.

The fat librarian at the desk was reading a copy of *People* magazine. I could tell from upside down the article she'd turned to was about the actress Liz Taylor and how she'd lost weight. It must've been an interesting article, because the librarian didn't even look up when I asked where I could find books on musical instruments.

"Playing, history or building of ?" she asked, turning a page.

"Um . . . playing."

"Seven eighty-seven."

"Excuse me?"

"Seven eighty-seven. Dewey Decimal System."

"Oh. Right. Where is it?"

"Third stack down, turn left and look in the middle

15

on the right. Got it?" she said, her nose still stuck in the magazine.

"Um . . . I think so." I didn't, but I didn't feel like asking her to show me, and besides, she looked like she could really use Liz Taylor's help. So I wandered around for five minutes until I found the right shelf, and when I did, my mouth fell open. There were rows and rows of books about playing musical instruments. I didn't know which ones to look at first. I read off the titles to myself. Some of them made sense—like *Playing the Guitar* and *Never Be Timid With a Trumpet*. But others were weird—*You and the Bassoon*, *The Celestial Celeste* and *Change-Ringing*. I thought the last one was about cash registers and that someone had put it on the wrong shelf, so I pulled it out to give to the librarian. But it turned out to be about playing church bells, so I put it back.

I walked up and down the aisle. I was getting nowhere fast. I couldn't look through all those books. My head was starting to feel fuzzy. Suddenly, I remembered something Buster once told me: "When good planning fails, trust Fate." Okay, Fate, I need your help now, I thought. I closed my eyes. "Eeny meeny miny mo," I whispered. I reached out and grabbed the first book my hand landed on. I opened my eyes and looked at the title. *Oompah-pah*, it said, and underneath, in smaller letters, *Tales of the Tuba*. There was a picture of the instrument on the cover. It looked kind

16

of big. But I decided to take the book out anyway and give Fate a chance.

When I got home, there was a package waiting for me.

"It just came," my mom said. "It's from C. Brown. Who's that?"

"Buster," I said. "His real name is Clovis."

"No wonder he changed it," Mom said.

I ripped off the paper. It was a book. *The Adventures of Robin Hood*. "Wow!" I yelled. I flipped through the pages. There were even pictures in this book.

My mother looked over my shoulder. "Didn't you read that already?"

"This is a different one. Buster said there are a bunch of books about Robin Hood," I explained.

Mom shook her head. "Lizzie, don't you want to read about something other than spiders or Robin Hood? How about *All-of-a-Kind Family* or *Little Women*? I loved those books when I was your age."

"Is *Little Women* the one with the wimpy kid who dies?" I asked.

"Beth March was *not* a wimpy kid. Her death was very sad. And anyway, how do you know about the book since you never read it?"

"You were watching a movie of it on TV last year, crying your eyes out. Just like Rona was crying over that dumb *Gone With the Wind*."

17

Mom threw up her hands. "How did I end up with a daughter with no romance in her soul?" she asked. But she laughed when she said it.

I went up to my room. I wanted to read my new Robin Hood book so bad I was almost twitching. But I knew I had to get right to work on solving Step A if I wanted to make sure Tessa didn't go to Pemborough without me.

So I took *Oompah-pah* out of my backpack and flipped through it until I found a chapter called "Advice for Beginners." I read part of it:

"The tuba is the largest and heaviest of all the brass instruments, hence it requires a fair amount of physical strength simply to manage the instrument and a great wind supply to play it. In addition, playing the tuba exerts stress on the face and abdominal muscles. A child should not begin to learn the tuba until he has achieved a certain degree of muscular development. He also should have his adult teeth—and those should be relatively straight and sound. And, of course, his mental development should be such that he can deal with the demands of lessons and practice. In general, it is not recommended that a child take up the tuba until he is thirteen years old."

I rapped on my skinny ten-year-old chest and stuck out my big buck teeth. "So much for Fate," I said, tossing the book across the room. I picked up *The Adventures of Robin Hood* and began to read it.

4

"Is this the voice of Gloriana, fairest maiden in Sherwood Forest?"

"Buster!" I yelled into the phone. He always calls me Gloriana—after the nickname of Queen Elizabeth I. "You're back!"

"No, my dear, I'm not. At least, I don't think I am. I seem to be where I last was."

I laughed. I was really glad to hear Buster's voice. I missed him.

"How are you, my dear?" he asked.

"Fine," I said. I wasn't really. I was worried. I now had only five weeks and five days left to learn an instrument. But for some reason I didn't want to talk about it—not even to Buster.

"Good. Well, Gloriana, I can't seem to reach my

niece today, so I thought I'd ask you to convey the message that I'll be over on Saturday to take her and her friend, Elizabeth, on an adventure."

"Whoopee!" I yelled. "That's great! I'll tell Tessa."

"Excellent. Tell Tessa I'll see her then. And tell her to tell Lizzie. Unless you want to tell her yourself."

I laughed again, said good-bye and hung up.

"Hey, sourpuss is smiling," Rona said, coming into the room.

"What's the big deal?" I asked, but the truth is, I knew what she meant. Two days had gone by since I'd made my bet with Tessa, and I wasn't any closer to winning it.

I stopped smiling. "I'm going up to my room," I said.

Ariadne waved two of her legs at me. I know a spider doesn't greet you like a dog does, but I think maybe Ariadne recognizes me. I took off the lid of her cage and rubbed her fuzzy back. "Ariadne, what should I do?"

Ariadne put two of her legs together. She looked like she was praying.

I couldn't help it. I started to smile again.

The water didn't look too deep. "Our horses can make it, Robin," I said.

"I trust thee, Elizabeth. Let us hold on tight."

We began to ford the stream. The water was up to our horses' knees, their bellies, their necks.

20

"Much deeper and we shall have to swim it ourselves," said Robin.

And then an arrow whizzed past his ear.

"Duck!" I yelled. And I fell with a splash into the water.

The arrows buzzed past my head like a swarm of bees, but I kept swimming. I made it to the other shore. "Robin, hurry!" I called, a second before an arrow struck me in the shoulder.

"Ouch!" I yelled, jumping off my bed. Something *had* stabbed me in the shoulder. I looked down. It was one of my mother's knitting needles. How did that get here? I wondered. Then I remembered that I'd used it to see if Ariadne would spin silk on it. She wouldn't. I put the knitting needle on my desk.

There was a knock on my door.

"Who is it?" I yelled.

"Rona."

I was so surprised that she'd actually knocked, I just said, "Come in."

She did, smiling sweetly and holding one hand behind her back.

I stared at her, wondering what she was up to.

"Ta-da!" she sang, holding out her hand. In it was her brand-new radio. "I just came to ask if . . . uh . . . I know you've been admiring my new radio, so I thought maybe you'd . . . uh . . . like to listen to it for a while," she said.

I kept staring at her. Either she was up to something

or she'd gone crazy. "Are you feeling okay?" I asked.

"Never felt better," she said. "So here. Take it. You can have it for the next forty-five minutes."

"Forty-five minutes?"

"Yes. Why don't you get comfortable? Lie down and use the earphones. They're really fun."

"Rona, what's going on?" I asked.

"Nothing's going on. You always tell me I'm not nice to you—so here, I'm being nice. Forty-five whole minutes worth of radio nice."

I sat on my bed and let her adjust the earphones. She turned on the rock station she likes. Then she said something, but I couldn't make it out.

I pulled one side of the earphones away. "What?"

"I said, 'Do you like it?' "

"Yes," I answered, still suspicious.

"Forty-five minutes," she said and walked to the door. She turned, waved at me and left.

I fiddled with the dial awhile, tuning in different stations. Music. More music. There were lots of different kinds of music, played by lots of different kinds of instruments. Except I didn't know what most of them were.

I listened to the radio for about half an hour until I realized I wasn't getting any further with Robin Hood or with my problem. I sighed, took off the earphones, got up and walked over to my window. I stuck my head out and took a deep breath. And then I noticed Rona, pacing back and forth on the patch of grass in front of our house. She kept looking at her watch, then up the street, then back at her watch. All of a sudden she stopped pacing, looked up the street once more, and stretched herself out on the grass. She sat up again and pulled something out of her pocket and opened it up. It was a fan. She stretched out again, propping herself up on one elbow, and began to fan herself. I couldn't figure out what she was doing. It wasn't even that hot. I watched her for a full minute, but she didn't budge. I shrugged, walked away from the window and went downstairs.

I decided to go to the library again. When I opened the front door, Rona was still fanning away. I shrugged again and started down the steps. Then I heard a squeaky sound, and I saw Toby Glickstein pedal into view on a delivery bike. He glanced at Rona, did a double take and brought the bike to a fast stop.

"Hey, hi," he said.

Rona didn't stop fanning. "Oh, hello, Toby," she said.

This time I did the double take. Rona didn't sound like herself. She had a funny accent. It sounded vaguely familiar.

Toby didn't seem to notice. Or if he did, he didn't mention it. Instead, he asked, "What are you doing here?"

"I live here," she answered in the same funny accent.

"I've . . . got . . . I mean . . . um . . . did you order a pizza?"

"Yes," she said. Only it came out "Yay-es."

I snorted. Rona hates pizza. She says it's greasy and fattening.

Toby got off his bike, opened the wooden crate attached to the back of it and took out a pizza box. "That'll be four dollars and thirty cents," he said.

Rona gracefully sat, then stood up. She snapped the fan closed and reached into her pocket. "Here's five dollars. Keep the change."

"Oh, no. I don't need a tip from you," Toby said. He held out the box.

"Course you do. I know you're such a hard-workin' man," Rona said. She tapped him with her fan, put it in her pocket and put the money into Toby's shirt pocket. Then she took hold of the other side of the box.

They stood that way, both of them holding the box, for a long time. I wondered if I should time them, for scientific purposes, when Toby finally let go of it.

"Um, Rona, I get off work at six. There's a free concert down at the park at seven. Maybe you'd, um, like to come with me. . . ."

"Why, Toby, I'd *love* to come," Rona said.

And then it hit me. The accent. She sounded just like a character in the movie *Gone With the Wind*, the one she was crying over. The character's name was . . .

"The only thing is, I have to take my little brother along," Toby continued.

I snapped my fingers. "Got it! Scarlett O'Hara!" I said out loud.

Toby and Rona both whirled around. "Oh, hi, Lizzie," said Toby.

But Rona didn't say a thing.

She just stared at me with eyes sharper than the Sheriff of Nottingham's sword.

"Say," said Toby, who couldn't see Rona's eyes at that moment, "maybe Lizzie would like to come, too."

I was about to refuse when I thought, A concert. Musical instruments. Just what I need to solve my problem. I closed my eyes so I didn't have to see Rona and said, "I'd like that."

"Great! I'll pick up my brother and meet you both at the entrance to the park at six-thirty, okay?"

"Okay," I said.

"Okay," mumbled Rona through clenched teeth.

"Great!" said Toby again. He got on his bike and rode away.

Rona spun toward me. "You little insect-loving tomboy, why didn't you stay upstairs listening to the radio?" she yelled, losing her accent. "My first date and you ruined it. I hate you! I hate you!" She threw the pizza at me and ran back into the house.

26

Luckily she missed. The broken box lay on the grass with the pizza oozing out of it. I shook my head. No matter how often I tell her, she still doesn't remember that a spider isn't an insect.

5

Rona wouldn't talk to me the whole way to the park. "Look," I said, "I'll sit far away from you and I won't look at you at all, so you and Toby can kiss each other all you want. . . ."

Rona let out a yell and raised her fists.

"Hello, Lizzie. Hello, Rona," someone called out. It was Mr. Jackson, the art teacher at the school I go to, wearing shorts and riding a motor scooter.

Rona dropped her fists and looked at him the same time I did. It was funny to see him in shorts, even though it was a hot July day and that was just what he ought to be wearing.

"Oh, hello, Mr. Jackson," Rona said in the Scarlett O'Hara voice she'd used on Toby. She used to have a crush on Mr. Jackson. It sounded like she still did.

The light turned green, and off he rode. I waved good-bye to him.

Rona turned to me again. "Don't say another word to me, Lizzie. Not one more word. I want to forget you exist." She began to walk faster, so that she was ten paces in front of me.

I stuck my tongue out at her back. Then I sighed. I don't know why Rona and I can't stand each other. I don't think it's because we're sisters, though. I don't think we'd get along if she were my twenty-third cousin I saw once a year. Mom says we'll get to like each other better when we get older. But I think the older we get the *less* we'll like each other, because that's what's been happening for years. I thought Rona was great when I was seven and she adored me when I was four. It's been downhill ever since.

Pretty soon we got to the park. Toby was waiting for us at the entrance just like he said he would be. With him was a chubby, freckled kid a couple of years younger than me. He wore heavy glasses, and his hair stood up in short wisps on top of his head.

"Hi, Rona, hi, Lizzie. This is my brother, Marshall," said Toby.

Marshall nodded at both of us; then he sneezed. And sneezed. And sneezed.

"Are you okay?" I asked.

"Ya-choo," sneezed Marshall.

Marshall sneezed a total of thirty-two times. I know

29

because I counted. I wondered if he had beaten the *Guinness Book of World Records*. I decided to look it up when I went to the library next.

He finally stopped sneezing and blew his nose. "Okay, let's go now," he said, walking into the park.

I walked next to him. Rona and Toby were ahead of us.

"Allergies," Marshall explained. "Grass. Pollen. This always happens when I go to the park."

"Then why did you come here?"

Marshall stopped dead and looked at me through his thick-lensed glasses like I was crazy. "Are you kidding?" he asked.

"No," I answered.

"It's a New York Philharmonic concert. And it's free, no less."

"They're good, huh?"

"You've never heard them?" he asked in disbelief.

"No."

He stared hard like I was from Mars or something. "Then how come you're here?"

"I . . . uh . . . I want to learn an instrument," I said.

"Which one?"

"That's what I'm hoping to find out," I mumbled. Then I asked, "Do you play something?"

"I play violin," said Marshall proudly. "I've been playing it since I was six. My teacher says I'm a prodigy."

I didn't know what prodigy meant, so I made up my

31

own definition that fit Marshall's personality. But I have a feeling it wasn't the right one.

We were at the bandshell. "Let's sit here," Toby called, pointing to a spot on the grass.

"Not here," said Marshall. "The acoustics aren't so good on this side."

"Okay, you tell us where to sit," said Toby, a trace of annoyance in his voice.

It took Marshall ten minutes to pick the spot. He tried out several different places, listening carefully to the musicians who were on stage tuning up while he did. Rona, Toby and I just stood and waited. Finally, Marshall motioned for us to join him.

Reluctantly, I sat down next to him. Toby was on my other side. "I like classical music a lot," he was saying to Rona.

"Oh, so do I," Rona, sitting next to him, said without her accent. I guess she gave up on it. "I listen to it all the time."

I pulled out a tissue and blew my nose to cover up my laughter. Rona's radio was permanently turned to WDEF—twenty-four hours of solid rock and roll.

"Who's your favorite composer?" Toby asked.

I waited to hear how Rona was going to deal with this one.

She hesitated like she was giving the matter serious thought. Finally she said, "I really can't pick one. There're too many good ones."

"You're right," said Toby. "There sure are."

I thought I heard Rona give a faint sigh of relief.

"There's an ice-cream cart," Toby said. "Let's get something."

"Okay," said Rona.

Toby turned to me and Marshall. "You guys want anything?" We shook our heads. "Save our seats for us, okay?" said Toby.

I nodded, but Marshall said, "There's a long line at that cart. You better get back before the concert begins. I don't want you interrupting my appreciation."

"Don't worry, Marsh. We'll be back on time," Toby said.

After they left, Marshall and I sat there in silence for about five minutes. I was thinking that Marshall was obnoxious, but he obviously knew an awful lot about music. I hated to ask him for advice, but I swallowed my pride and said, "Marshall, I need some help. Could you help me? Could you tell me about the different instruments?"

He looked at me and asked, "Do you like classical music?"

"I've hardly heard any," I answered truthfully. "Just what my friend Tessa plays on the piano sometimes."

"Then why do you want to play an instrument?"

I didn't want to tell him the truth, so instead, I asked, "Do you have to like classical music to play an instrument?"

33

"It helps—unless of course you're interested in playing some other kind of music, like jazz or rock." I swear he turned up his nose when he said that.

"I like rock," I said.

"I figured you would," said Marshall.

Snotty little brat, I wanted to yell, but I didn't want to make a scene. Besides, I really did need his help.

More of the orchestra began to dribble onto the stage. A man was carrying a thing that looked like a pipe with a handle. A woman was lugging the biggest violin I'd ever seen. She set it down on the floor *between her knees* and started playing it.

"I might like classical music once I get to hear it," I said.

Marshall didn't respond to that, but in a friendlier voice he said, "That's Irma Siricki. She teaches at the music school I go to."

"That woman with the giant violin?"

"It's not a giant violin. It's a cello," Marshall said in a boy-are-you-dumb tone.

"And that funny pipe thing, what's that?"

"A bassoon," he said in the same tone.

Another musician walked onstage carrying his instrument.

"That's a flute," said Marshall.

"I know that's a flute. I'm not ignorant!" I snapped. "Are you going to keep making fun of me? Do you like it when people make fun of you, which I bet they do all the time?"

Marshall blinked at me. And all of a sudden he looked just like the little kid he was.

I felt bad and said softly, "Marshall, I really do need your help. I *have* to learn to play something. I just have to. And I won't know what to play if I don't know what there is to play. Will you help me?"

Marshall thought a moment. "Okay," he said.

We smiled at each other.

Then he ruined it by adding, "But you better listen carefully. I don't want to have to repeat myself." He cleared his throat and began to explain to me about the four major sections of an orchestra—strings, wood-winds, brasses and percussion. I listened carefully, waiting for the answer to my problem.

I didn't hear anything that was really helpful when he went through the first three sections. But then he got to percussion.

"Percussion instruments are the ones you bang, beat, hit, etc., like the drums, cymbals, chimes and all that stuff they give you in school to play—triangles, blocks, tambourines and such."

I began to get excited. The triangle. I could play that. Anybody could play that. If I could get into Pemborough as a triangle player . . .

But Marshall punctured my idea fast. "Percussionists are different from the other musicians in the orchestra because they have to know how to play *all* of those instruments," he said.

I sighed.

35

"Any questions?" Marshall finally asked.

I thought a minute. "What about the piano? What kind of instrument is that?"

"Good question," he said approvingly. "The keys are attached to hammers that hit the strings, so it's both a percussive and a string instrument."

The whole orchestra seemed to be onstage now, tuning up. "Anything else you want to know?" Marshall asked.

"Yes. Which is the easiest of all those instruments to play?"

Marshall shook his head. "I can't answer that. It depends. . . ."

"On what?"

"On your own aptitude or ability."

I asked him, "How can I find out what my aptitude is?" But he didn't get to answer, because just then Toby and Rona came back.

"Here we are, right on time, just as I promised. I'm Toby-on-Time," Toby said.

Clutching an ice-cream bar, Rona giggled like he'd said the cleverest thing in the world.

Suddenly a round of applause went up from the audience. The conductor had come onstage.

"Shhh," ordered Marshall. "Lizzie, try to listen to each of the instruments."

We shut up. I tried to do what Marshall told me to, but it was hard. I didn't know what I was listening for. I tried to decide if I had more aptitude for banging, bowing or blowing an instrument, but I honestly didn't know.

Eventually the concert ended. "Wonderful. Just wonderful," said Marshall. "Wasn't it, Toby?"

"Yeah. It was. That pianist might become another Vladimir Horowitz," he answered. "Don't you think so, Rona?"

"Definitely," she agreed, stifling a yawn.

Rona once told me that whenever she was bored, she sat and thought about hairstyles that would look good on her. I wondered how many new hairstyles she'd come up with during the concert.

Marshall turned to me. "Well, what did you think?"

"It was good," I said weakly.

Marshall stood up. "I'm going to talk to the first violinist. Oh, before I forget . . ." He took out a pad, scribbled something down on it and handed it to me.

I looked at it. " 'Le Conservatoire de Musique, 59 Willow Ave.' Hey, that's near my house. 'Mr. Jasper.' What is this?" I asked.

"The school I go to. Go see Mr. Jasper. He might be able to tell you what instrument you'd be best suited for. He's tough, but good."

I looked up, pleased. "Hey Marshall, thanks. If there's anything you ever want to know about spiders or Robin Hood . . ."

Marshall waved his hand as if to say "Forget it" and walked away toward the stage.

6

"Why are you so jumpy today?" Tessa asked.

"I'm not jumpy," I said too quickly, pacing around Tessa's room. I didn't want to tell her that as soon as she started her piano lesson, I was going to see Mr. Jasper. I was pretty sure he could help me—but I was nervous, too. It was weird not telling Tessa about my feelings. I always used to.

I went over to her dresser, picked up a fancy mirror and made a face into it.

"For somebody who's not jumpy, you're doing a pretty good imitation," Tessa said.

I put the mirror down. "I wonder where Buster's taking us tomorrow. Maybe he found an archery range nearby. Wouldn't that be neat?" I chattered, still pacing.

"Lizzie . . ."

"I bet you'd be good at using a bow. You've got strong hands from playing piano."

"Lizzie . . ."

"I've been trying to make my arms stronger. I started doing push-ups like this—"

"Lizzie! You're making *me* jumpy."

I looked at my watch. "Hey, it's time for your piano lesson. I better go."

Tessa looked puzzled. "But Ms. Gerard isn't even here yet."

"She'll be here any minute. She's always on time, isn't she?"

Tessa gave me a funny look. "Whatever you're up to, Lizzie Silver, I hope it's worth it."

I stopped pacing and looked at her for a long minute. "It's worth it," I said.

I could see something click in Tessa's brain. "Oh," she said softly.

We were so quiet, we both could hear a car pull up. "Ms. Gerard," I said. " 'Bye. See you later." I charged out the door.

I was trying to act calm as I walked up the steps to *Le Conservatoire de Musique*. But it was hard. I felt so nervous, my stomach was flopping around inside.

The school was an old building—brick with ivy crawling up one side—but not run-down. I climbed the steps and took a deep breath. Then I opened the door and walked in. I knew I had to find the main office. Schools always have some kind of main office or another. I headed down a narrow hall. From a room at the end I heard voices—a loud female one and a softer male one.

The woman boomed, "We absolutely must do something to increase enrollment, Karl. A repeat of an incident like that last one could ruin us. If we don't, the school will go under."

"The student was unbalanced, Beryl," the man answered.

"The student was sensitive, Karl. You need to encourage your students more. Your students show the highest dropout rate."

"Are you saying I'm not a good teacher?"

"You're an excellent teacher," Beryl said. "But you're too demanding."

"We are supposed to be turning out virtuosi here. I drive my students hard so they will be great," Karl said stiffly.

"They won't even be competent, let alone great, if they all try to smash up their instruments like the last one did."

I was near the room now, and just as I got to the door, Beryl came barreling out, slamming the door behind her. She was as big as her voice. She bumped right into me, and for some reason, I apologized. I started to ask where the main office was, but she was

40

already halfway down the hall.

I shrugged and walked on. Finally I found it. It wasn't called Main Office. It had a sign that said "Registration." I remembered when we moved to Brooklyn that my mom had had to register me in school, so I guessed I was on the right track here.

I went into the Registration room. There was a woman in a flowered dress sitting at a desk there. She would've been pretty if she hadn't looked so frazzled. "What now?" she asked. "I mean, how can I help you?"

I took another deep breath. "I'm Lizzie Silver," I said, "and I'd like to see Mr. Jasper."

"You sure of that?" the woman said.

I blinked at her.

"I mean, do you have an appointment?"

"No, I didn't know I needed one."

"You do. Unless Mr. Jasper is by some chance free, which I'd be surprised if he was, especially right now. But I'll check anyway. Have a seat." She went out.

I sat down. The chair was hard and uncomfortable. I glanced around the room. It was painted what my mom would call a "restful green." There was a desk, with a sign on it that said "Ms. Cafferty" and a typewriter, and some more chairs. On the walls were a couple of posters of men with long, curly hair. I figured they were musicians, but I didn't recognize any of them.

After checking out the room, I looked at my hands.

42

My mom always talks about how Tessa has the hands of a pianist. I wondered what kind of hands I had. The hands of a bassoonist? Or a violinist? Or a tubist? I couldn't tell, but I sure hoped Mr. Jasper could. I was glad I'd cleaned my fingernails that morning.

Ms. Cafferty still hadn't returned, so I took out my new Robin Hood book from my backpack. I'd already read half of it. I opened it to a new chapter. It was called "Robin Hood Meets Allan-a-Dale." Who's he? I wondered. I turned the page and there was a picture of him. Underneath it was written "Allan-a-Dale, Minstrel." He looked young and handsome, but what caught my eye was what he was holding in his hands. It was a pretty little harp.

"That's it!" I said out loud. "Robin, you've saved the day!"

Just then, Ms. Cafferty came back in the room. "I'm glad you're in a good mood," she said, "because I'm afraid Mr. Jasper can't see you right now."

"That's okay," I said rapidly. "I don't need to see him anymore. See, I didn't know what instrument to play and I wanted him to tell me which one I've got an *ap-ti-tude* for. But now I know, so I'll just sign up for lessons instead."

"Hold it, hold it," said Ms. Cafferty. "Let me get this straight. You don't need to see Mr. Jasper. You just want to sign up for lessons now."

I nodded.

43

"What instrument?"

"The harp."

She looked bug-eyed at me. "The what?"

"The harp."

"Did you say 'the harp'?"

I wondered if she was hard of hearing, so in a loud voice, I said, "THAT'S RIGHT. I WANT TO PLAY THE HARP."

She winced and covered her ears. "Hey, I'm not deaf."

"Sorry," I said.

Then she put her hands down and asked, "Do you know Corrie Greenblatt?"

This time I stared at her. "Who's Corrie Greenblatt?"

But before she could answer, a booming voice behind me said, "Is there a problem here, Ms. Cafferty?"

Ms. Cafferty jumped, then straightened her collar. "Oh, Ms. Bronson. I didn't hear you come in. We have a new . . . er . . . student."

Ms. Bronson came over to me. "Hello. You look familiar."

It was Beryl. I didn't tell her she'd bumped into me ten minutes ago.

"What's your name?" she asked.

"Lizzie Silver."

"And what is it you'd like to study?"

"The harp," I said.

Her face became blotchy. "Did Corrie Greenblatt put you up to this?" she asked, clenching her fists.

"She says she doesn't know Corrie Greenblatt," said Ms. Cafferty.

The place was crawling with crazy people. I stood up, looked at my watch and said, "Uh-oh, I'm going to be late. Thanks for—"

"Just a minute," said Ms. Bronson, blocking my way. "You wish to learn the harp?"

"Um . . . yes . . . the harp."

"Why?"

"Well, er . . ." I didn't want to tell her about my bet, so I said, "Because Allan-a-Dale did."

"Who?"

"Allan-a-Dale. Robin Hood's minstrel."

She began to smile. "Ah. You like Robin Hood."

"And she doesn't know Corrie Greenblatt," Ms. Cafferty repeated.

Ms. Bronson suddenly seemed to relax. "Well, let's see now. You can have lessons Monday, Wednesday or Friday from eleven to twelve. Which day would you like?"

This time I didn't answer her question. Instead, I asked, "How long will it take me to play the harp?"

"That depends—"

"On my *ap-ti-tude*," I finished for her.

She beamed at me. "Quite correct. And on how much you practice. But I would say, if you take a lesson a week and practice an hour a day, you'll begin to play with some facility in two or three months."

"Two or three months! That's too long!" I blurted out.

Ms. Bronson gave me a funny look. I thought she was going to ask if I knew Corrie Greenblatt again, but instead she said quickly, "Of course, if you practice often and take more than one lesson a week . . ."

I thought about it. If I took three lessons a week and practiced two hours a day, that might do it. I was just about to say that to Ms. Bronson when another thought hit me. "How much are lessons?" I asked.

"Fifteen dollars an hour. Plus the cost of renting the harp for practice, which is five dollars an hour. Unless you own your own harp, of course."

I shook my head. "How much does a harp cost?" I asked.

"About ten thousand dollars," said Ms. Bronson.

I gulped. "I think I better rent one."

She smiled and nodded.

I did some more figuring. If I took three lessons a week that would come to forty-five dollars. If I practiced two hours a day, that was five times two times five or fifty dollars. Fifty plus forty-five equals ninety-five dollars. Ninety-five dollars! I gulped again. I knew my mom and dad would give me some money for music lessons—Mom'd been after me to study an instrument for a long time. But they wouldn't give me ninety-five dollars. Thirty-five maybe, but not ninety-five. I sighed. What if I only practiced an hour each day, but practiced hard? That would come to twenty-five instead of fifty dollars, plus forty-five . . . "Excuse me a minute," I said to Ms. Bronson, and I took a pad and pencil out of my backpack. I wrote down the numbers. Seventy dollars. That would be seventy all together times five weeks. Three hundred and fifty dollars. My parents would give me half that. Where could I get the other hundred and seventy-five? Let's see. I had about eighty-five dollars in the bank, which I'd been saving to buy a microscrope, and I was earning eighteen dollars a week feeding animals for Markham the Magnificent. He's a magician and I feed his animals. Buster got me the job to pay for Ariadne, and I still have it. Eighteen times five came to ninety dollars (minus two dollars for Ariadne's crickets). Eighty-eight plus eighty-five is one hundred and seventy-three dollars. I sighed again. Bye-bye microscope.

"Okay," I said to Ms. Bronson. "I'd like to sign up for three lessons a week, plus one hour of practice time each day."

"Three lessons! My, what a determined girl you are!" boomed Ms. Bronson. Then she said, "Do you have a deposit?"

I looked in my pocket. All I had was two dollars.

"That'll do," said Ms. Bronson, practically snatching it out of my hand.

Ms. Cafferty produced a form of some kind. "Sign here," she said.

I did.

"Your parents will have to sign this one." She handed me another form.

I put it in my backpack.

"I can tell you're going to be a marvelous harpist," said Ms. Bronson.

"You can?" I said. "You mean I have harpist's hands?"

Ms. Bronson looked at them. "Yes, indeed."

"Oh, that's great!"

"Well, I must go back to my office. See you on Monday, dear."

"Uh, Ms. Bronson, one more thing."

"Yes?"

"Who's my teacher going to be?"

"Mr. Jasper," said Ms. Bronson.

"Mr. Jasper! That's great!" I exclaimed.

Ms. Cafferty and Ms. Bronson gave each other funny looks.

"You . . . er . . . know him, dear?" asked Ms. Bronson.

"No, but I was going to see him for an aptitude test today."

"Until she figured out she wanted to play the harp," Ms. Cafferty added.

"Marshall says he's tough, but good."

"Marshall? Do you mean Marshall Glickstein?" asked Ms. Bronson.

"That's right," I said.

"Ahh," said Ms. Bronson. She and Ms. Cafferty looked at each other again as if they knew something I didn't.

"Well, see you Monday," Ms. Bronson said once more and left.

"Good-bye, Ms. Cafferty," I said.

"Good-bye and good luck," said Ms. Cafferty.

Just as I got to the door, I thought I heard her say, "You'll need it."

7

"I'll get it! I'll get it!" I yelled, rushing to the front door. I was at Tessa's, and I guess she should have opened her own door, but I was so excited, I didn't care about being polite. I opened the door so hard it banged against the wall.

There was nobody there.

"Huh?" I said.

Then, slowly, a hand appeared from the side. In it was a single red rose.

I started to laugh.

And Buster, looking handsome in a white shirt and jeans, jumped out. I threw my arms around him and gave him a hug. "He's here, Tessa!" I called.

"So, Gloriana, are you and my niece ready for an exciting and daring adventure?"

"Is it your new way to wake up people?"

"Perhaps."

Tessa walked into the hall, followed by her mother.

"Come on, Buster, give us a hint," Tessa said.

He thought a minute and said, "Let's say that this adventure was inspired by Robin Hood."

"Whoopee! I bet I know what it is," I said, thinking of the archery range.

"I hope whatever it is doesn't involve stealing," Tessa's mom said, and yawned.

"My dear sister," said Buster, "it involves RO-MANCE." He handed her the rose.

"My mom says I don't have a drop of romance in my soul," I said.

Buster looked at me. "Forgive me, my dear, but your mother doesn't know a hawk from a handsaw. Anyone who likes dashing adventures certainly has a drop of romance in her soul. In fact, I'd say she has at least a quart."

We all laughed. Then Buster, Tessa and I piled into his car and away we went.

I couldn't stop smiling. Everything was going right. We were on an adventure with Buster. On Monday I would start learning to play the harp and stop Tessa from going to Pemborough alone. And in the book I was reading, Robin Hood had just bumped off the evil Guy of Gisborne.

Buster must've felt my good mood, because he started to sing:

51

Alas, my love, you do me wrong
To cast me off discourteously,
Though I have loved you so long,
Delighting in your company.
Greensleeves was all my joy,
Greensleeves was my delight,
Greensleeves was my heart of gold,
Oh, who but my Lady Greensleeves?

When he finished singing, I applauded hard. "That was wonderful," I said.

Even Tessa agreed. "Yes, it was. Sing some more."

He did.

I leaned back in my seat, feeling happy, and watched the trees flash by. They got thicker and thicker until they seemed like a forest. Sherwood Forest. I closed my eyes and pretended I was riding through it on a horse instead of in a car, with Robin riding at my side.

Soon I heard Buster's voice say, "And now, fair damsels, your carriage has arrived."

I opened my eyes and looked out the window again, right at an enormous sign that said *Medieval Faire, Sherwood Forest*. We turned into an enormous parking lot full of cars. "Sherwood Forest! This isn't an archery range," I said out loud. "Is 'faire' with an e the same as 'fair' without?"

"It is," said Buster.

"Great!" I yelled, scrambling out of the car. "Which way in?"

"One moment, Gloriana, Tessa," Buster said, getting out. He opened the trunk of the car and took out a pair of boots. Leaning against the fender, he stooped down and untied his sneakers. I wondered why he was changing comfortable sneakers for hard-soled boots when the next thing I knew he'd started to take off his pants.

"Buster, what are you doing?" Tessa gasped.

I didn't say anything. I just looked at the blue tights he had on under his jeans and the white shirt with the big sleeves he was still wearing and I started to smile. When he slipped on the boots, took a dark-red tunic out of the trunk of the car and put it on, my smile became a grin.

"What does *medieval* mean?" I asked, even though I had a feeling I knew.

"From the Middle Ages."

"When Robin Hood lived?" I asked.

"Exactly." Buster plopped a floppy blue hat with a feather on his head. "Well, how do I look?"

"Don't ask," muttered Tessa.

"Like . . . like a poet," I said.

"Excellent. I shall be perfectly in place."

I wasn't sure what he meant, but I was getting more and more excited.

"Now, follow me," Buster said.

Tessa looked longingly at the car. For a minute I

53

was afraid that she was going to refuse to be seen with us. But she sighed, stiffened her back the way she does when she has to do something she doesn't want to do and followed us to the entrance. There we saw other people, in costumes like Buster's, buying tickets. Buster paid for the three of us, and in we went.

And as soon as we did, I saw just what Buster had meant. Spread out before us was a huge park with a lake in the middle of it and wooded hills surrounding it. Off in the distance was a bridge. On the grass were men and women in velvet and satin gowns, tunics and doublets. They wore fancy hats and headdresses. Some carried swords and shields, daggers or bows and arrows. Others held flutes and drums or baskets of flowers and fruit. Many of them were setting out their wares in stalls dotting the park. Right near us two women were dancing with tambourines, a man was juggling bowling pins and a red-haired boy about my age, dressed in a suit with a red-and-black diamond pattern all over it, was turning cartwheels. And all over the place were signs that read: "REWARD: £25 for the capture of Robin Hood." It looked just like a scene from a movie. Except I was in it.

"Buster! This is fantastic!" I shouted.

And Tessa said, "You should have told us beforehand, Buster. Then we could've come in costume, too."

Buster and I looked at each other and grinned. We

54

both know Tessa's a sucker for beautiful dresses.

"Sorry," he apologized. "Next time I will. But I wanted this to be a surprise. . . . Here's the program of today's events. There's a lot going on that's not on the program, too." He handed one each to me and Tessa.

"Oh, there's a Maypole Dance at eleven-thirty," Tessa said, reading hers. "That'll be pretty."

I looked at mine. "Mud Pit at noon. What's that?"

"Mud wrestling, I think," said Buster, grinning.

"Great!" I said.

"Ugh!" said Tessa, squirming.

I checked out my program again. " 'Twelve-thirty, Squire's Tale. One o'clock, Costume Pageant. One-thirty, Puppet Show. Two o'clock, Lyrical Lutes' "— I almost choked at that one—"'Two-thirty, Robin Hood Meets the Giant at the Bridge.' Robin Hood! Wow! What time is it now?"

"Eleven-ten. Can you hold out that long?"

"I don't know," I said.

Buster and Tessa laughed at me, and I joined in.

"Where to first?" asked Buster.

"I'd really like to see that Maypole Dance," Tessa said. "And the Maypole's right over there."

I didn't much care to, but I decided to be nice. "Okay," I said. "Save me a place. I'm going to get a soda."

I headed toward a nearby stand. And the next thing

55

I knew, I was lying on the ground.

" 'Ey, why doncha watch where yer goin'," a voice with a funny accent said.

I sat up and blinked at the boy who'd been turning cartwheels. His red-and-black tights were ripped at the knee and his belt was crooked. But he was grinning at me.

"Why don't *I* look where I'm going?" I said. "You knocked me down."

"Sorry, I'm sure." He held out his hand and pulled me up. "Are you 'urt?"

I brushed myself off. "No."

"Good." He held out his hand again.

"What's that for?"

"This is for me tip."

"Your tip? For what?"

"For being a gent and 'elping you up."

"Get lost," I said.

He shrugged, not only with his shoulders, but with his eyebrows, too. Then he did four back somersaults. With the last one, he knocked someone else down, this time a heavy woman. I watched as he helped her up and stuck out his hand. I saw the woman laugh heartily and put a coin on his palm. I couldn't believe it. "What a crook!" I said out loud. "Wait'll I tell Tessa and Buster about this guy."

I forgot about my soda and hurried back to the May-pole. I found Buster and Tessa. "You'll never believe

this kid I just met. He—" I began.

But Tessa said, "Shh. It's starting."

I turned my head. A bunch of people in gorgeous costumes were marching to the Maypole. They each grabbed the end of a brightly colored ribbon and began to dance in and out, twining the ribbon around the pole. Tessa was right. It was pretty. But I didn't pay that much attention. I was waiting for two-thirty and Robin Hood.

Buster and I left Tessa watching a magician while we went to see the mud wrestling. These three guys insulted each other and rolled around in the mud. It was great. Then we rejoined Tessa and had lunch. Buster was right about there being a lot of things going on that weren't on the program. There were people walking around singing or telling stories or dancing. Just as we finished eating, three people, a man and two women, came over to us and started singing. Buster jumped up and joined them.

"In spring time, in spring time, the only pretty ring time," they sang. "When birds do sing, hey ding a ding a ding, sweet lovers love the spring."

The song was kind of corny, but they sure sounded good, especially Buster, whose high voice blended in just right. People started to gather around and listen. I looked at Tessa. She was smiling.

The group stopped singing and started clapping Buster

on the back. "Excellent! Superb!" they said. "Do you sing professionally? Do you play an instrument?"

Buster shook his head. "Not I. I am a poet."

"A poet you may be, but you are also a singer. Come join us," the man said to Buster.

He shook his head. "Not now. I must escort these fair damsels to yon puppet show."

"Go ahead with them, Buster. Just meet us by two-thirty at Robin Hood's bridge," I said. "We'll be there at two to get good seats."

"Are you sure you don't mind my going?" Buster asked, looking from me to Tessa and back again.

"We're sure," we both said.

"All right." He waltzed away with the other singers.

Tessa and I finished our sodas and wandered around for a while. We looked over the game booths and the stuff for sale. Then, just as we were about to head for Robin Hood's bridge, a familiar funny voice rang out.

" 'Ey, miss. Are you still too cheap to 'elp an honest acrobat earn a day's wages?"

I whirled around.

It was the boy in the diamond-patterned suit. He was sitting on a platform over a tank of water. There was a sign in front of the tank that said: *Dunk the Fool*.

" 'Ere. For a mere shilling—that's a quarter to you— you can knock me into this 'ere bucket. Isn't that worth digging into yer pocket, or do you only spend money on Mondays and Thursdays?"

59

I giggled and realized his voice, his accent, reminded me of the Artful Dodger. He was this boy crook in a movie I saw called *Oliver!*

There was an older boy standing at the booth. He turned to the Artful Dodger and said, "Maybe she needs a reason to dunk you."

"Aww, she probably couldn't hit the side of a castle with a melon from one foot away," the Artful Dodger sneered. Then he looked at me and stuck out his tongue.

Tessa came over to me, "What's going on?" she asked.

I didn't answer her. "Who says I can't?" I demanded.

"I do, ya bandy-legged brat," the Artful Dodger cat-called.

"Oh yeah?"

"Lizzie, what's going on?" Tessa asked again.

"What's going on is that I'm going to Dunk the Fool," I said. I handed the older boy a quarter and he gave me three balls.

"Pitch 'em at that circle. If you hit it, down he goes," said the boy.

I closed one eye and took aim. I missed by a mile.

"Ha-ha. Told you she couldn't do it," jeered the Artful Dodger.

The small crowd watching us started to laugh.

I pitched the second ball real fast. This time I was even farther off.

"Methinks she needs an eye doctor," said the older boy.

"Methinks she needs a relief pitcher," said the Artful Dodger.

"Want to try it blindfolded?" the older boy said.

"Or how about with both hands tied behind your back?" said the Artful Dodger.

Everyone laughed again.

"Get him, Lizzie," Tessa cheered.

"May the force be with you!" someone else yelled out.

The crowd was really whipped up now. I tried to concentrate, gave up, closed both my eyes and threw the ball as hard as I could. I heard a thump, a creak and a splash. A roar went up from the crowd. I opened my eyes, and there was the Artful Dodger up to his neck in water.

"Hooray!" people cheered. "Give the gal a trophy!"

The Artful Dodger scrambled out of the tank and, vaulting over the edge, landed at my feet. He held out his hand. " 'Alf a crown," he said.

"For what?" I asked.

"Damages to me clothing," he said, holding his wet suit away from his body.

"I paid to get you wet and now you want me to pay to get you dry? No way."

" 'Ave a 'eart. 'Ow am I going to show meself to me mother looking like this?"

I didn't even think. I just said, "Tell her you were felled by Elizabeth Silver of Sherwood Forest. If she hasn't heard of me yet, she soon will."

"Elizabeth Silver! *The* Elizabeth Silver!" He staggered back.

I tried not to laugh. "Be off with you, or my friend Robin and I will give you something worse than wet pants," I said, wishing I had a sword in my hand to wave at him.

"I'm a-going, I'm a-going," he said, walking backward.

I stood there until he was all the way to the tank. Then I walked away. But before I was too far to see him, I turned my head once. He was sitting on his platform again. He waved at me. I waved back and hurried on to see Robin Hood.

8

By the time we got there, there was already a bunch
of people sitting on both sides of Robin Hood's bridge.

"Which side should we sit on?" Tessa asked.

I studied the wooden footbridge. Then I felt a tug
at my leg. I looked down. A chubby man was sitting
there.

"Sit on this side. I've seen this show before, and take
my word for it, this is the best view."

"Gee, thanks," I said.

"Don't mention it."

Tessa and I plunked ourselves down next to the
chubby man, as near to the bridge as we could. "Ooh,
I can't wait," I said.

"Like Robin Hood, do you?" the man asked.

"Oh, yes," I answered. "Very much."

"Bet you'd like to be his Maid Marian."

"Not really," I said. "She doesn't get to do very much."

Then Buster appeared. His cheeks were a little pink and his eyes were bright. "What ho, beauteous maidens!" he called, climbing over assorted pairs of legs to get to us.

I scrunched nearer to Tessa so Buster could sit down. "Did you have fun?" I asked him.

"Yes, indeed," he said. "And you?"

"Lots," I said.

Suddenly, a murmur rippled through the crowd. I turned my head. Two men in brown tunics and high boots were striding toward the bridge, followed by a small man all in green.

"Oh," I gasped. I couldn't believe it. He was just the way I'd pictured him—slim and handsome, with long brown hair and a pointed beard. The only difference was that he didn't have his bow and quiver of arrows. Instead he had a sword in his belt and a staff. And when he started speaking in what Buster called a "melodious" voice, I wanted to jump up by his side and be in Sherwood Forest with him.

"Friends, upon this bridge we will part," he said. "I will tarry here awhile."

"Good Robin, they say near this bridge does dwell a giant of a man who takes not kindly to strangers," said one of the men in brown.

"No man, be he giant or dwarf, does frighten me. Let him accost me if he dares."

The men in brown left. Robin laid down his staff and sat on the bridge, dangling his legs over the side. And then the "giant" appeared. He wasn't really a giant, but he was pretty big, and he had a long wooden staff in his hand.

"Stand, sir, and return whence you came," he commanded in a deep voice.

"Sir, my way lies forward, not backward."

"Your way will lie beneath the ground if you heed not my words."

"Here is my reply to your words," Robin said. Quick as a spider catching a fly, he drew his sword and lunged at the giant, who held up his staff and beat back the blow.

The fight was on. Up and down the bridge they fought. The audience was yelling, "Get him, Robin" and other things until the giant's voice rang out over the crowd. "Fie, sir, metal against wood? I must needs remedy that," he said. And he knocked the sword from Robin's hand.

The audience gasped. The big man charged at Robin. Robin stepped backward. His foot touched his own staff. He kicked it up into his hand. Everyone cheered. The battle was on once more. Staff clashed against staff. Finally, Robin got his across the giant's neck.

"He's got him!" I shouted. I was so caught up in

the fight that I forgot I knew the outcome from the books I'd read. "Come on, Robin. Wallop him!" I yelled.

But the big man flipped Robin over his back like a sack of laundry—a *light* sack of laundry. Robin dropped his staff. The giant kicked it away, held Robin over his head and spun around.

"Oh, no!" I moaned.

"Let us see how well you like the underside of my bridge," the giant said. And with a heave, he threw Robin over the side—our side.

Robin somersaulted gracefully and landed in the water. The giant panted and laughed.

I couldn't laugh. I jumped up, and before Tessa or Buster could grab me, I jumped over people's feet, hopped over the rope separating the crowd from the bridge, ran out on the planks, picked up Robin's staff and hit the big man right across the rear end. He staggered and reeled around to stare at me.

My eyes got big, and suddenly I remembered where I was. I clapped my hand over my mouth.

"Sit down, little girl," the giant hissed at me.

"I'm sorry," I whispered, and fled the bridge. I stumbled over pairs of legs back to my seat while the whole audience laughed at me. I couldn't look Tessa or Buster in the face.

Robin, laughing, crawled up the bank to the bridge. He didn't seem to be hurt. "Friend, give me your hand.

So fair a fighter I never have seen. What be your name?" he said to the giant.

The giant didn't answer. He was too busy wincing.

"I said, 'What be your name?' " Robin repeated.

The big man shook his head. "Uh-humph. I be John Little," he replied. "And who are you, brave sir?"

"I am called Robin Hood."

"Robin Hood! For many a year have I longed to meet you. Let me join your merry band, and your loyal servant will I be."

"That I will, and gladly, too. But you must have a new name. We will call you Little John. Do you not find that fitting?" Robin slapped him on his rear end.

"Oww," said Little John. "You clod!"

The crowd laughed again.

Robin repeated his question.

"Most fitting," Little John said through clenched teeth.

"Let us to the greenwood go," said Robin. He almost landed another slap on Little John's bottom, but the giant got out of the way and hurried across the bridge. Laughing, Robin followed him. When he was near me, he looked down and said loudly, "Anytime you care to join my Merry Men, you're in." He winked and strode away.

The people around me laughed. I felt my stomach shimmy and my face get hot. I didn't say a thing.

Neither did Tessa or Buster, but I could tell Tessa

was pretty embarrassed for me. I knew I should be embarrassed, but somehow I wasn't. Not anymore. Robin had liked what I'd done. He'd thought it was great.

And I knew right then and there that I was going to take Robin up on his offer—by hook or by crook.

9

"I have to meet him," I said. It was Sunday, and Tessa and I were in my room. "I have to. He even asked me to."

"Lizzie, he asked you to join his Merry Men," Tessa said.

"That's the same thing."

"He's an actor. He was acting."

I sighed. "Tessa, I know he's an actor," I said, "but he's . . . he's the closest person to Robin Hood I've ever seen."

"Why, Elizabeth Ann Silver, I do believe this is your first crush," she teased.

"It's not a crush," I said.

"I can see the headlines now," Tessa went on. " 'Girl Switches from Spiders to Robin Hood: "It's Not a Crush,"

she says. "It's True Love." ' "
"Tessa, that's mean."
She smiled. "You're right. I'm sorry. . . . Okay, I'll help you."
"Great!" I got out a big sheet of paper.
"We don't have to make a chart this time," Tessa said.
"We don't?"
"No. I think you should write a letter to Robin."
"A letter?"
"Yes. Telling him how you were the girl who tried to save him from Little John, that you enjoyed his performance so much you just got carried away."
"And that I want to join his Merry Men," I interrupted.
"No," said Tessa.
"No?"
"No. He's not going to write back and say, 'Aye, aye.' "
"Why not? He asked me—"
"Lizzie," Tessa said gently, "he was having fun with you."
"He wasn't making fun of me."
"Not *making* fun. *Having* fun. Playing. Acting, like I said before."
We were quiet a minute. Then I said, "Well, what should I tell him so I can meet him?"
"Let me think," Tessa said.

71

While she was thinking, I took out the stationery Mom got me for my last birthday. It's light blue and it has a unicorn in the right-hand corner. I'm not interested in unicorns. I'm only interested in animals that are real. But Mom doesn't understand. She thinks all girls my age love unicorns. It's no use trying to tell her it isn't true.

"That's so pretty," said Tessa as I lifted out a sheet of paper. "Will you write me letters on it?"

I felt my chest get tight, but I said calmly, "Why should I write you letters when I see you every day?"

Tessa didn't answer me. She just fiddled with the hem of her dress.

"I guess I could write you from Vermont if we go there on vacation again."

Tessa smiled at me. It was a nice smile, like she liked me a lot.

I felt my eyes get wet a little. I turned my head to the paper. "All right. How about if I just write what you said and then tell him I want to meet him."

"No. It's not . . . special enough. You've got to impress him somehow."

"I've already impressed him," I said.

But Tessa ignored me. "I've got it. Write this down."

I picked up my pen and unicorn stationery.

"No, on scrap paper first."

I got some and Tessa began to dictate:

" 'Dear Robin Hood, My name is Lizzie Silver—' "

72

"Elizabeth," I said.

Tessa gave me a funny look, but she said, " 'Elizabeth Silver. I am the girl who tried to save you from Little John yesterday. You see, I am a great fan of Robin Hood. In fact, I am studying him for a special project. I would like to meet you and discuss this project. Please let me know when this would be convenient. Thank you. Sincerely yours, Elizabeth Ann Silver.' "

"Tessa, I'm not studying Robin Hood."

"Sure you are. You're reading all the books about him, aren't you? That's studying."

"No, it isn't. It's . . . it's . . . enjoying. Enjoying and studying are two different things."

"Look, Lizzie, I'm only trying to help," Tessa said, losing some of her patience.

We both got quiet. After a long pause I said, "How about this: 'Dear Robin Hood, I am the girl who tried to rescue you from Little John yesterday. I'm ready to join your Merry Men except for one thing—I don't know how to use a bow and arrow. Maybe you could give me lessons. Please write to me and let me know when I can meet you. Thank you. Sincerely yours, Elizabeth Ann Silver.' "

Tessa started to laugh.

"What's so funny?" I demanded.

"Your letter," she said, still giggling. "I don't think Robin Hood's got the time to give you archery lessons."

"Thanks a lot, Tessa Lawrence. I don't laugh at you," I said.

"That's because I never . . . do anything . . . worth laughing at," Tessa teased in between giggles.

"Miss Perfect!" I snapped.

But it only made Tessa laugh harder. Soon I started to laugh, too. When I stopped, I asked, "What's wrong with my letter? Is it dumb?"

Tessa shook her head. "It's cute, but I don't think Robin Hood's got time to give you archery lessons."

I sighed. "You're probably right. Well, what should I write?" I said, throwing up my hands. And all of a sudden it came to me. The only problem was I didn't want to tell it to Tessa. I grabbed the stationery.

"What are you writing?" she asked.

"Uh . . . what you told me," I lied. "About the special project."

"I thought you didn't like that."

"No, it's fine," I said, writing quickly.

Tessa gave me another funny look.

"Could you open the window? It's stuffy in here," I said.

Tessa did. I finished the letter and folded it in half.

"Do you want me to check the spelling?" Tessa asked.

"No," I said, shoving the letter into the envelope and sealing it. "Where do I send it?"

"To Robin Hood, care of the Medieval Faire, Sherwood Forest."

"What's the address?"

"It's on the program we got."

I addressed the envelope. "Let's mail it right now. I'll get a stamp from Mom," I said.

"You mail it, Lizzie. I promised to do some errands for my dad." Tessa got up and left.

I knew she was annoyed at me. I didn't blame her. I felt bad about lying, too; but it would've spoiled everything if I had told her what I really wrote, because what I wrote was:

Dear Robin,

My name is Elizabeth Silver. I am the girl who tried to save you from Little John yesterday. You asked me to join your Merry Men. I want to very much. I think I'd be a good Merry Man. You see, I play the harp, just like Allan-a-Dale.

Please tell me when I can come and join.

Thank you.

Sincerely,
Elizabeth Ann Silver

If anything'll impress him, I thought, that will, and I ran out to mail the letter.

10

I was sitting in Ms. Cafferty's office again, but this time I was feeling more confident. I was going to have my first harp lesson, and I knew it was going to be great. I knew that for two reasons: 1) I wanted to play the harp; 2) Ms. Bronson had told me I had harpist's hands.

Ms. Cafferty was busy blowing her nose and swallowing Vitamin C. "Subber code," she said. "De worst kide."

"You know, there are some other animals besides humans that need Vitamin C," I said.

"Yeah? Like whad? De elephad? A code would sure ruin his day."

"No. Like the guinea pig," I answered.

"It figures," said Ms. Cafferty.

Suddenly, from somewhere else in the building,

there was a loud bang and somebody started to shout, "I've had it. That's it. I quit! I never wanted to learn piano anyway. And certainly not from a creep like you."

"Uh-oh, here we go again," said Ms. Cafferty, getting up and going over to a cabinet.

More voices joined in outside. They sounded like they were arguing or pleading or something, but I couldn't hear what they were saying.

"No! And I'm not coming back!" the first voice yelled.

I heard the distant slam of a door. Ms. Cafferty pulled a file out of the cabinet. After a few minutes, Ms. Bronson came into the office. "I'm afraid Joel Mafrena will not be studying here anymore. He wants a refund on the classes, too. I'll have to see his file. . . ."

Before she even finished speaking, Ms. Cafferty handed it to her.

"Why dote you fire hib?" Ms. Cafferty said, and blew her nose again.

"After this I may have—" Ms. Bronson began, then noticed me. "Ah, the girl who signed up on Friday, Lizzie Gold."

"Silver."

"Beg your pardon?"

"Lizzie Silver."

"Oh, of course. And you're going to study . . . ?"

"The harp, with Mr. Jasper."

Ms. Bronson went blotchy. "Oh yes, of course. Mr.

78

Jasper will be . . . er . . . a few minutes late today. Perhaps you'd . . . er . . ." She looked at Ms. Cafferty.

"You read bovie bagazines?" Ms. Cafferty asked.

"No," I said. "Could I look at my harp while I'm waiting?"

Ms. Bronson gave a big sigh of relief. "Oh, of course, my dear, come right this way."

She took me to a small room. In the middle of it there was a big thing covered with cloth. She whipped off the cloth. And there was a harp a million times the size of Allan-a-Dale's. "But how can I carry it around?" I said.

"Ha ha. Very amusing," said Ms. Bronson.

"No, I mean it. Allan-a-Dale's harp was only this big." I motioned with my hands.

"Ah, you mean the *Celtic* harp. We teach only the *orchestral* harp here. But I'm sure you'll enjoy playing it."

I was wondering if I should get my deposit back and find a school that teaches the Celtic harp when, as if she were reading my mind, Ms. Bronson said, "No music conservatory in the neighborhood teaches the Celtic harp."

I sighed and walked over to the big harp. It was beautiful—tall and golden. I ran my fingers across the strings. There were a lot of them, and they sounded heavenly.

79

"It is lovely, isn't it?" said Ms. Bronson.

I ran my fingers across the strings again. Harpist's hands, I thought.

"If you like, you may sit here and wait for Mr. Jasper."

"I'd like that," I said.

Ms. Bronson smiled and left.

I sat down next to the harp. I looked it over, and I saw that there were pedals on the bottom of it. Seven of them. I wondered what they did. I pressed one of them down, but nothing happened.

Then I noticed another interesting thing. The harp had a little leather purse hanging from it. I didn't think it would hurt to open it, so I did. I reached inside and felt two things—a piece of paper, and something hard made out of wood and metal. I took both things out. The wood-and-metal thing looked like this:

I turned it over in my hand a few times and put it back in the purse. I was going to open the paper when it fell out of my hand on the floor near the harp. I got down on my hands and knees to pick it up.

"Interesting position, but I'm afraid the harp is not played that way," a voice said. It was a strange voice—dry, like brown leaves.

I jumped, bumping my head against the harp and almost knocking it over. It seemed like people were always catching me in weird positions.

I stood up, red in the face, and saw in front of me the thinnest man I'd ever seen. Everything about him was thin—his nose, his lips, his hair.

"I . . . I dropped something. A piece of paper. It was in that purse."

"That is not a purse. That is a tuning-key holder. And in the future I'd prefer it if you do nothing to this instrument unless you have been instructed to do so. Is that clear?"

I nodded my head.

"Good. Then we shall get along just fine." He smiled, and even his smile was thin.

"Now, what is your name?"

"Lizzie Silver," I said.

"I am Karl Jasper. I shall call you Miss Silver. You will call me Mr. Jasper."

I nodded again, even though he hadn't asked me a question.

"Have you ever played the harp before?"

"No," I said.

"Have you ever played *any* instrument before?"

I thought hard. Finally I said, "Sticks—in second grade."

"Sticks?"

"They looked like sticks. They were made of wood,

and they were thick and smooth—"

"Claves," he said.

"Huh?"

"You played claves. Always refer to things by their proper name."

"Yes," I said, and, for some reason, I added, "Sir."

"Well, Miss Silver. We have no evidence of any musical talent on your part. But neither do we have evidence of any lack of it. You may become one of the great harpists of our time."

I blinked at him. "Really?" I said.

"It is possible. . . . Now, we begin. Lesson One, First Section: Parts of the Harp. Sit in that chair, Miss Silver, and listen carefully."

I did.

"This is an orchestral harp. It became truly orchestral when the pedals were added. The harp consists of forty-seven strings, each attached to the neck at the top with its own tuning peg and to the sound board at the base, and seven pedals that sharp or flat the notes." He walked around the harp, pointing to the various parts. When he finished, he said, "Repeat what I have just told you."

I did.

"Good. We go on to Section Two: The Correct Position of the Harp. Listen, but do not move. The harp, when in use, rests on the player's right shoulder and inner knees. It is inclined toward the player so that

83

only these two feet remain on the ground. The *player's* feet must be flat on the floor—never hooked around the chair legs, Miss Silver—and the player's body must be neither too tense nor too relaxed. The chair should be placed so that the player has easy access to all the strings. Is that clear?"

"What about the player's arms?" I asked in a low voice.

"Speak up, Miss Silver."

"What about the player's arms?" I repeated, louder this time.

"The arms, Miss Silver, will be discussed later. Let us see how well you have absorbed what I have said so far. Let us see you place your instrument in the correct playing position."

I swallowed hard and stared at the harp. It shouldn't be too difficult, I said to myself, as I moved the harp. Sit straight, lean it back . . .

"Miss Silver, are you planning to play that harp or burp it? Begin again."

I spent the next fifteen minutes learning to hold the harp. Finally, Mr. Jasper said, "Good. Section Three— now we add the arms." He said I had to hold them absolutely horizontal. "*Wrists in, elbows out* is the key," he said. "All right, Miss Silver. It is your turn. Do not pluck the strings. Just hold your arms like so. . . . No, no, no, stop humping your shoulders. You are not Quasimodo ringing the bells, Miss Silver."

I tried to stop humping my shoulders, but then I dropped my elbows.

"Again, Miss Silver."

I tried. And tried. And tried until my arms ached.

"Have you not been taking your vitamins, Miss Silver? Well, let us proceed to Section Four: Fingering." He showed me how to use my thumb, index, middle and ring fingers to pluck the strings. "Thumbs are placed in an upright position, like so. After you pluck, you must release the fingers against the palms. Like so. Now, you see that thick red string in the center of the harp? That is middle C. Put the fourth finger of your right hand against it. Let your other three playing fingers rest on the next three strings. Now pluck. No, no, no. Your thumb must be upright. . . . Watch that elbow. . . . Stop humping your shoulders. . . . Again."

I was getting tired and my shoulders were really hurting bad, but I tried once more.

Mr. Jasper frowned. "I believe you have practice time coming up next, Miss Silver. I suggest you use it. Your lesson is finished for today."

I would have jumped out of my chair with joy— except I was too tired. "Mr. Jasper, will I be able to play a song soon?" I asked.

"A song? Be happy, Miss Silver, if you will soon be able to pluck a string correctly. Good day."

He left the room, and I leaned my head against the harp. This was going to be harder than I thought. I sat there quietly for five minutes. Then I rubbed my sore shoulders. I had an hour of practice ahead of me.

I found out that an hour is a lot longer than I thought. Plucking the same string over and over is pretty boring. In fact, after ten minutes I stopped and had a great daydream about Robin Hood. I went back to plucking for a while, and then I had another daydream. The daydreams were fun, but the truth is that by the end of the hour, I was feeling a little discouraged. Would I really be able to play the harp in five weeks?

When I got outside the school, I stuck my harpist's hands into my pockets and felt a piece of paper in one of them. I pulled it out. It was the paper that had been stuck in the tuning-key holder. Slowly, I unfolded it. There was a message written on it. It said: "I hope your head gets stuck in the strings. Corrie Greenblatt."

I looked up from the note just in time to see Marshall Glickstein hurrying past me, his violin case in his hand.

"Marshall!" I called.

He stopped and squinted at me.

"Lizzie. Lizzie Silver. We went to—"

"I remember," he said, coming over.

"Do you know who Corrie Greenblatt is?" I asked him.

"Everybody at *Le Conservatoire* knows who Corrie Greenblatt is. She tried to smash her *harp* over Mr. Jasper's head. She didn't succeed, of course."

"I was afraid it was something like that," I said, showing him the note.

"Where'd you find that?"

"In the tuning-key holder of my harp."

"Your harp?" he said.

"I'm studying the harp with Mr. Jasper."

He started to laugh. It wasn't a nice laugh. "You're studying the harp with Mr. Jasper? You sure opened a can of worms. Ha ha."

"What do you mean, a can of worms? You're the one who told me to go to Mr. Jasper, who said he was tough, but good."

"I told you to go to him for an aptitude test. I never told you to study with him. I wouldn't study with him in a million years. He's a maniac. Ha ha." He walked away.

"Thanks a lot, Marshall," I yelled after him. "Thanks a lot."

I heard him laughing all the way up the street.

11

"There is a faire in Nottingham town today, and I propose to go," said Robin. "I intend to win the archery contest there."

"That is not wise," Friar Tuck spoke up.

"You will be captured," said Little John.

"Nay, I think not, for I will dress as a monk. And I shall take a guard with me."

"Who will you take?" asked Little John.

Robin's blue eyes looked around. "I shall take the bravest of all my Merry Men—I shall take Elizabeth."

I jumped to my feet. "And I shall be happy to go. Do I need to dress as a monk, too?"

"No, Elizabeth. You will dress as a gentle maiden, so no one will guess your strength."

"How clever!" I said. "And I shall hide my sword under the skirt. But where will you get my clothes?"

"Here is a dress Maid Marian has lent you. Put it on while I tend to the horses. We must leave at once!"

"At once!" I repeated, taking the dress—just as the phone rang downstairs.

I opened my eyes and looked at my clock. It was nine o'clock. I sighed. In just two hours I had another lesson with Mr. Jasper, and this time I wasn't looking forward to it too much.

"Lizzie!" my mother called. "It's for you."

I sighed again and went to the phone.

"I'm going shopping today with my mother. Want to come?" Tessa's voice said. "We're leaving in an hour."

I was glad she had called. We hadn't talked to each other the day before, and I figured she was still annoyed at me. But I couldn't go shopping with her and miss my lesson. "I can't," I told her, without saying why.

"Oh" was all she said.

There was a silence. Then she said, "Robin probably got your letter today."

I felt my heart thump. "Yeah. He probably did. How fast do you think he'll write back?"

"That's hard to say," said Tessa.

Another silence. I was starting to feel bad again. "Want to go for a sundae later?" I said.

"Mom's taking me for one after we go shopping. But how about a swim at the pool at three? It's hot today."

"I've got to feed Markham's animals at three-thirty."

"Oh, that's right. I forgot."

89

"But I'll be finished by four-thirty," I said. "We could take a swim then."

"I can't. I've got my piano lesson."

"I forgot."

"After that I'm going to a concert in the city—the one we got tickets for months ago."

"Oh," I said. "I guess I'll see you tomorrow then."

"Tomorrow I'm going to my grandparents' house again."

"How's your grandmother?"

"A lot better. . . . Look, I've got to go, Lizzie."

"Wait," I said. "How about Friday?"

"That looks okay. Want to come here at eleven?"

"Uh . . . no. I'll come over at one-fifteen."

"One-fifteen?"

"Yeah. I'm busy in the morning."

"That means we'll only have two hours together until you have to go to Markham's."

"I guess so," I said.

"Lizzie, what's going on?" said Tessa.

"I can't tell you," I said.

"Does it have anything to do with our bet?"

I wondered whether or not to tell her the truth.

"Does it?" she asked again.

"Yes," I finally said. "But I'm not going to say anything else."

"Oh, Lizzie," said Tessa. "I hope you know what you're doing."

So do I, I thought. But what I said to Tessa was "I do. See you Friday at one-fifteen."

I didn't walk as fast to *Le Conservatoire de Musique* as I had on Monday. In fact, I kind of dragged my feet. Tessa wasn't the only person who'd invited me to do something that morning. My dad came into the kitchen while I was just finishing breakfast and said, "Lizzie, I'm taking the day off today. I thought maybe you'd like to go to the Aquarium. We haven't been there together in a long time."

"I can't, Dad," I said, really miserable. My father and I don't get much of a chance to do things together. He found out how sad I was about it, and he's been trying to fix things up when he can. And now it was my fault we couldn't. "I've got my music lesson."

"What music lesson?"

"Didn't I tell you, David?" said my mom. "Lizzie's taking music lessons. Isn't that wonderful?"

"That is wonderful, Lizzie. But a music lesson doesn't take up the whole day."

"I've got to practice after the lesson. At three-thirty I've got to go to Markham's."

Dad smiled at me. It was a sad smile. "My busy Lizzie," he said.

"Lizzie's becoming very responsible," said my mother. "And mature."

Then Rona came into the kitchen in a long T-shirt

that came down to her knees.

"I don't suppose *you'd* like to hang out with your old man today?" Dad asked her.

Rona gave him a look like he'd asked her to eat chocolate-covered ants or something.

"Rona's seeing her *young* man today," Mom teased.

"Oh, Ma," Rona said, annoyed.

"Toby Glickstein is a nice boy. And very smart," Mom said.

Rona mouthed the words as Mom was saying them. I laughed. Instead of laughing with me, Rona gave me an annoyed look.

It was definitely turning out to be, as Mom would say, "not my day."

I left soon after. I was two minutes late for my lesson, which I would never have known if Mr. Jasper hadn't pointed it out.

"Two minutes may seem like an insignificant amount of time to you, Miss Silver, but timing is of the essence in music and in life. I trust you will not be late again."

"No, Mr. Jasper."

"Good. Lesson Two. Let us first see how well you have remembered what you learned on Monday."

I moved my chair into position.

"Closer, Miss Silver," said Mr. Jasper.

I obeyed him.

"Wrists in, Miss Silver. Watch those shoulders. Now, play C. . . . No, no, no. Not so—enthusiastically.

Pluck it with more delicacy."

"Like this?" I asked, gently plucking the string.

"I said delicately, not anemically, Miss Silver. Again. . . ."

"My fingers feel sore, Mr. Jasper."

"I'm sure they do, Miss Silver, but that will cease when you learn to pluck the strings properly. . . . All right. Now it is time for theory."

"Theory?"

"Yes, theory."

For practically the whole rest of the lesson, Mr. Jasper told me about theory. He talked about staffs and measures; clefs; whole, half and quarter notes; rests and Every Good Boy Does Fine. He drew strange squiggles on a funny blackboard with lines on it. He pointed at the harp and talked some more about scales and octaves and key signatures, which he said were not like tuning keys because I asked him if they were and that I shouldn't worry about them right now anyway. When he finally finished talking, my head hurt and I felt dizzy.

"All right, Miss Silver. Look at this." He drew something on the lined blackboard. "What note is this?" he asked.

I stared at the blackboard. It was all blurry. "I . . . I . . ."

"I'm waiting, Miss Silver."

"I can't remember, Mr. Jasper."

"I see I shall have to go over this again next time.

93

Your lesson is over for today, Miss Silver. Here's your theory homework for Friday."

"Homework?"

"Of course, Miss Silver. This is a school. Good day."

As soon as he left the room, I started to cry. My head hurt, my fingers hurt, and I was going to spend an hour hurting them some more. I'd missed chances to be with Tessa and my dad. I was nowhere near playing a song either, and I had less than five weeks left to learn one well enough to win my bet.

I sat there feeling sorry for myself until I thought of Robin Hood—out in the forest, fighting for survival, starving sometimes, getting wounded other times. He wouldn't cry over a headache or some sore fingers. And when he became an outlaw, he had to give up seeing a lot of his friends, too. I wiped my eyes. I leaned the harp back against me in the right position, stuck my elbows out and wrists in, held my thumbs upright "like so" and began to practice. I knew Robin would've been proud of me.

12

I tripped up Tessa's steps and practically fell against her doorbell. I heard the bell ring, but no one opened the door.

I looked at my watch. One-twenty-three. Tessa couldn't have left yet. She wasn't like Mr. Jasper—she wouldn't mind my being eight minutes late. Especially if she knew the reason I was late, which was that Mr. Jasper had changed my Friday lesson time, just for that day, from twelve to one, instead of eleven to twelve, and he'd kept me late practicing my first song, which I'd hoped was going to be something classy like Tessa plays but turned out to be "Mary Had a Little Lamb." And that took me forever to learn. I still couldn't play it well by the end of the lesson.

"I'm trying to do it right, Mr. Jasper," I'd said, exasperated.

He looked at me with eyes like pieces of ice. "There is no such thing as trying, Miss Silver. There is merely doing and nondoing. If you wish to play the harp, you will do so correctly or not at all."

He made me play it again, and all of a sudden I understood just how Corrie Greenblatt must've felt. I wanted to pick up my harp and smash it over Mr. Jasper's head until he saw little birds tweeting around him like a cartoon bad guy who'd just gotten zapped. I was glad when the lesson was over and I could get right out of there and not have to stay to practice.

I rang Tessa's bell a second time. Still no answer. She wasn't mad at me anymore, was she? I tried the bell once more. Then I sat down.

I sat there for half an hour, but nobody ever answered or showed up.

Slowly, I walked home.

I opened the door to my house and went in, heading for the living room. "Mom!" I called. "Did Tessa . . ." I stopped dead.

Rona and Toby were sitting on the sofa with their lips locked tighter than a cricket wrapped up in Ariadne's silk. They sprang apart as soon as they saw me, like someone had unplugged them. Toby banged his knee against the coffee table and groaned.

Rona gave me one of her Get-Out-of-This-Room-Fast looks.

I ignored it. "Did Tessa call?" I asked.

"Nobody called," she growled.

"Where's Mom?"

"Shopping."

"Was there any mail for me?" I knew it was too early to get a letter from Robin, but I asked anyway.

"No," she snapped.

"Okay." I turned, and as I walked out of the room, I said, "You can go back to kissing now."

Rona threw a pillow at me and missed.

I got to my room and slumped down on the bed. Where was Tessa? What had happened? I was worried. Even if she was angry at me, she wouldn't do something like not be there when we'd made plans. Suddenly this nasty thought came to me. Pemborough. It has something to do with Pemborough. That's why she didn't call. She didn't want to tell me what she was doing.

Wait a minute, I told myself. Tessa's not like that. She wouldn't cancel and not call you.

But the nasty idea was growing. Maybe she thought she was being kind by not telling you. Maybe she didn't want to upset you like she did the other day when she asked you to write to her. Maybe she's even accepted Pemborough without telling you and you're wasting your time trying to learn the harp from mean Mr. Jasper. . . .

I was getting so worked up, I had to stop myself. Whoa, Lizzie, there's probably another perfectly logical explanation why she didn't call. You can call her later and find out.

98

But I was still feeling upset as I stretched out on my bed. Calm down, Lizzie, I told myself. Calm down. Robin wouldn't get upset like this. Close your eyes and think about riding with him to Nottingham Faire and the archery contest.

But I couldn't. I felt too bad. I got up, deciding to take a walk before I had to go to Markham's. I flung open my door, and as I did, Rona, who was on the other side of it, came flying into the room.

"Did Scarlett O'Hara come into people's rooms without knocking?" I asked.

"I was just going to knock," Rona said.

"Sure you were. . . . But I'm not going to argue with you today. I'm in a hurry."

"Lizzie, can I talk to you for a minute?"

Something in her voice made me stop and look at her. "Where's Toby?" I asked.

"He went home."

"How come? I thought you were going out for ice cream."

"I told him to go. I said I had something else to do."

"Why'd you do that? I thought you liked Toby."

"I do like Toby. A lot."

I waited quietly for her to go on.

She did. "He likes me, too."

"So what's the problem?" I asked gently.

"The problem is he's smart. Very smart, as Mom says. Much smarter than me. I . . . He talks about all these things and people, like just now he was talking about Valdimir Horowitz—"

"Vladimir."

"See, even you know who he is."

"I don't, but Toby mentioned him at the concert the other day. He said he's a pianist, and he must be a good one because—"

"Enough, Lizzie. You don't have to make me feel dumb, too."

I stopped. After a pause, she went on, "Anyway, if I tell him I don't know what he's talking about, he'll know how dumb I am and he won't like me anymore." And then my big sister burst into tears.

I felt weird. I went over to her, and I guess I should've hugged her or something, but we haven't hugged in a long time. So instead I just patted her back. "You're not so dumb," I said. "You know a lot of stuff."

"What st-stuff d-do I know?" she blubbered. "I d-don't know about c-classical music. Or c-computers. Or R-Robin Hood—"

"Toby likes Robin Hood?"

Rona nodded. "H-he saw your b-book on the c-coffee table and said it was one of his f-favorites when he was a kid. He liked the way Robin dressed as a m-monk to go to the fencing contest—"

"Archery contest."

"Archery contest. And he said he always wanted to fight the Sheriff of Buckingham."

"Nottingham. Rona, you could find out about Robin Hood easily. You can read my book. I'll lend it to you. Then you could talk to both me and Toby about it."

Rona wiped her eyes and looked at me. "I could?"

"Sure."

She thought a minute. Then her eyes narrowed. "What do you want in return?" she asked.

"Nothing," I said.

"I don't believe you."

"I mean it, Rona. You can borrow my book anytime you like—free of charge."

Rona stood up awkwardly. "Gee, thanks, Lizzie." She started for the door. Then she turned. "I lied to you before. Tessa did call."

"She did?" I shouted.

Looking ashamed, Rona nodded. "Yes. About an hour ago. She said her grandmother got her cast off, tripped and hurt her other ankle. They were taking her to the hospital. She said if she can't see you later, she'll see you tomorrow."

I felt relief go through me, because Tessa hadn't told Pemborough she was coming, and then I felt ashamed that I was relieved. Poor Grandma Brown had hurt herself. You're not a nice person, Lizzie Silver, I thought.

"I'm sorry I lied," Rona said.

I stopped telling myself off and looked at Rona.

We smiled at each other, and I left to go to Markham's.

13

Markham has a big old house with rickety steps and a library full of books about magic. I rang his bell. He wasn't there, so I let myself in with the key he gave me and headed straight for Sparkle. She's a boa constrictor and my favorite of all Markham's animals. She'd eaten a mouse only yesterday, and she was very sleepy. I didn't want to bother her, so I didn't pet her. The rabbits—Flopsy, Mopsy, Cottontail and Peter—were rattling around in their cages. So was Little Flower, the skunk, and even the doves, Lavinia, Fritzi and Josie. They always know when I'm there to feed them even before I go into their room. They're a lot more intelligent than people think.

"Okay, okay, I'm coming," I called, going to them. "Let's see, what's on today's menu? How about some yummy mixed grain, followed by some tasty oyster-shell grit?"

While I was feeding them, Buster came in. He has a key to Markham's, too; he uses the library a lot.

"Hello, Lizzie," he said, quietly sinking into a chair in Markham's backyard.

"Buster!" I said, glad to see him.

He didn't look or sound as cheerful as he usually does. I suddenly realized that Tessa's grandmother is his mother. "How's Grandma Brown?" I asked.

"Accident prone," he said. "She'll be all right. It wasn't a break this time after all—merely a sprain." He ran a hand over his face.

I wanted to do something for him—he looked so tired and pale. "Can I make you a cup of tea?" I asked.

"Thanks, Lizzie, but I had three cups in the emergency room."

He didn't say anything for a couple of minutes after that and neither did I, which was strange because Buster and I usually "talk up a storm," as my mom says. He just sat there with his eyes closed.

I finished feeding the animals, and when I turned around, Buster was still a little pale, but he looked less tired.

"Feel better?" I asked.

"Yes, thank you, Gloriana."

"Want to talk now?"

He laughed. "Certainly. What shall we talk about?"

"Have you figured out your new way to wake people up yet?"

His eyes began to sparkle. "Something is stirring in ye olde noggin," he said, tapping his head.

"What is it?" I asked.

"A Poem-In."

"A what?"

"A Poem-In. In the 1960's we had Love-Ins and Be-Ins. Maybe you've heard of them."

I nodded. My mom never went to any of them, but my dad went to a big Be-In in Central Park. He told us about it at dinner once. He said everyone got dressed in beads and bells and flowers and danced and sang and had a good time. Some of them took drugs, too, but my dad left out that part. I found it out from Tessa's mother, who also went to it (although she didn't know my dad at the time).

"Well," Buster continued, "at a Poem-In, a whole bunch of people go to a park with a poem to read. Which we do, amid dancing, singing and eating."

"And drugs?" I asked.

Buster laughed. "I hope not. I think that's one part of the sixties I'd like to forget. Anyway, then we all attach our poems to balloons and let them fly."

"That sounds great," I said. "But won't it take a lot of work to organize?"

"It could. Would you like to help me with it?"

"I don't know if I have the time," I said, feeling bad

104

because Buster's always helped me a lot.

He didn't get annoyed. Instead, he just said, "I understand." He didn't ask me any questions.

But I decided to give him more of an explanation anyway. "Buster, I want to tell you something, but don't tell Tessa. . . . I'm studying the harp."

"The harp! How lovely! What a delightful instrument!" he exclaimed. "But why don't you want Tessa to know?"

So I told him the whole thing—from our bet through the concert and Marshall all the way up to mean Mr. Jasper.

"I see," Buster said.

"But Buster, I don't know if I'm going to make it," I said, feeling the sadness come over me. "I mean, I don't know if I can play the harp well enough to stop Tessa from going to Pemborough this year."

He smiled gently at me and said, " 'Ah, but a man's reach should exceed his grasp, Or what's a heaven for?' "

Buster always quotes poems and parts of poems to me. Then I think about what he's quoted until it makes sense. I never liked poetry before Buster made it interesting. "Did you write that?" I asked him.

"I wish I had. But no, those lines were written by Robert Browning. Do you know what they mean?"

I thought about the lines for a long couple of minutes. Then I said, "You mean I should keep trying, even if I fail, don't you, Buster?"

He smiled again. "Right on the button, Gloriana. Do you know why?"

"Because that's the way to get to heaven?"

"Maybe. Or maybe because getting to heaven means trying to do something greater than you think you can do. It's being brave. It's rescuing Will Scarlett from the hangman—even though your own life is in danger. And it's people exploring the unknown—reaching toward the stars. Taking risks with life and with art."

"Like astronauts exploring outer space?" I asked.

"Yes, but also people exploring their own souls," said Buster. He closed his eyes and said, "That's true bravery indeed."

"You lost me."

He opened his eyes. "I'm feeling philosophical today, Gloriana. Please pardon the highfalutin ruminations." He laughed at himself and said, "You're a brave damsel, Elizabeth. And I salute you." He jumped up and did a fancy bow.

"Thank you, Sir Buster. You're a brave gentleman."

"May this brave gentleman escort this brave lady for a scrumptious hot fudge sundae?"

I patted my stomach and bravely said yes.

14

"Do you think I should write him another letter, Tessa?
Maybe he didn't get the first one. Mom's always com-
plaining about the mail—"

"Lizzie, it's only been a week and a half. He's probably busy. Actors work hard."

I nodded. But the thing is I kept forgetting he was
an actor. Or not really forgetting—it's just he was both
an actor and Robin Hood. It was all mixed up in my
mind. "Maybe I should've tried to call him instead,"
I said. "If he's *that* busy, maybe he doesn't have time
to write. Maybe I should call him now."

"How could you call him? You don't have his phone
number."

"I could call the Medieval Faire—there's a phone
number on our program—and ask to speak to him."

"I don't think they'd put him on the phone."

"I guess not," I said and sighed.

There was a pause, and then Tessa said gently, "Lizzie, could we do something today that doesn't involve Robin Hood? We haven't seen each other in over a week."

It was true. Something had come up every single day. First there was Grandma Brown's ankle. The next day, my dad decided the whole family was going to go away for the weekend "for a change."

When we came back, I was sure Tessa and I would get together on Monday, but instead *her* father decided her family should go away for a few days. So it wasn't until two whole terrible harp lessons later that we got together.

I answered Tessa, "Okay, we won't talk about Robin Hood today. What shall we do?"

Tessa thought a minute. "Let's go to the playground."

"The playground? At school?"

"Uh-huh."

"Why do you want to go there?"

"I don't know. I just do."

"Okay," I said with a shrug.

It was a hot day as we strolled over to the playground. I thought a swim was a better idea, but Tessa really seemed to want to go there.

The playground was deserted. With school out, nobody hung around there much. I sat down on one end of the seesaw. Tessa sat on the other end. We seesawed up and down, giggling like little kids. All of a sudden Tessa began to giggle harder.

"What's so funny?" I asked.

"I was . . . hee hee . . . just thinking of the time we . . . hee hee . . . went to see *Dracula* and you . . . ha ha . . . said the movie was unscientific . . . hee hee . . . because vampire bats don't suck blood from wounds, they . . . hee hee . . . *lap* it from wounds."

"Well, it *was* unscientific."

Tessa laughed harder.

I started to giggle, too. "What made you . . . hee hee . . . think of that anyway?"

"I don't know. . . . Oh, yes I do. We came here afterward, and we started making jokes about 'I vant to *lap* your blood' while we were seesawing."

"That's right. I remember."

Tessa stopped seesawing. "This place has a lot of memories," she said, sounding sad.

"Not really," I said.

We got off the seesaw and sat on these wooden climbing posts. After a moment Tessa said, "I saw Julie Lindstrom this morning."

"Lucky you," I said. Julie Lindstrom was my archenemy in class last year.

"She pretended she didn't see me, but I knew she did," said Tessa.

"I hope she won't be in my class this year."

"Yes."

We sat in silence. Then Tessa said, "Lizzie, I have to tell you something. Pemborough has offered me a scholarship."

I jumped up from the post. "You didn't tell them you were going yet, did you? You promised. You—"

"No, Lizzie. I didn't accept them yet. I just wanted to tell you—"

"Why? Why did you want to tell me?"

"Oh, Lizzie, come on. Be reasonable. I want to be a pianist. I've been offered a scholarship to one of the best music schools in the country."

"Tessa, you promised."

"I know I promised, and I won't go back on it either. But Lizzie, the chance of you winning that bet is—"

" 'Ah, but a man's reach should exceed his grasp, Or what's a heaven for?' " I yelled at her.

She blinked and stared at me.

"Why did you want to come to this playground? To see it onc last time before you go?" I turned and marched off.

But Tessa followed me. "Come on, Lizzie. Stop being so angry at me. Please? Come on. If you win the bet, then you can thumb your nose at me. If you don't win, let's not waste the time we've got left together in Brooklyn being angry."

I didn't answer her, just kept walking. She followed me right up the steps to my house, still begging me to stop being mad at her. I opened the door, and she followed me inside.

"Lizzie, will you listen to—"

"Oh, Lizzie, you're back. This just came for you," my mom said, coming into the hall.

She handed me an envelope and went out again. I stared at it. It was pale green and addressed to Elizabeth Ann Silver. There was no return address. Hurriedly, I ripped open the flap and took out a single sheet of pale-green paper. It said:

Dear Elizabeth Ann Silver,

So, it is you who attempted to rescue me. I thank thee most heartily. And thou art a minstrel as well. A minstrel is always welcome. I hereby dub you an official member of my Merry Men. You are now free to spread truth and justice throughout Sherwood Forest and adjacent lands.

Peace,
Robin Hood

"Wow!" I yelled. "Wow! He wrote! He wrote! He's made me a Merry Man!" I jumped up and down and, forgetting I was mad at her, threw my arms around Tessa.

"That's great!" she yelled back.

We both jumped up and down.

"Let me see it," Tessa said, taking the letter from my hand.

I let her read it. I was so excited I didn't even think about what it said.

"Girls, keep it down," my mother yelled from the

111

living room. "I'm trying to read."

"I'm a Merry Man!" I hollered again.

"And a minstrel," Tessa said, looking at me.

I stopped jumping up and down and looked back at her.

"Lizzie, you couldn't have written what I told you to write, so what *did* you write to him?" she asked.

I gave her what my mother calls a "sheepish" look. "I can't tell you," I said. "Not for three weeks."

Tessa sighed. "Okay, Lizzie. Okay. Just tell me we won't fight anymore today."

"Okay. We won't fight," I said. Then I yelled, "I'm a Merry Man," again. Now all I had to figure out was how to get to Sherwood Forest.

15

Things were definitely looking up. I got through another harp lesson and I didn't even cry after it. I spent the weekend with Tessa and we had a good time. Neither of us mentioned Pemborough at all. And I wrote another letter to Robin, all by myself.

Dear Robin, (I figured since he made me one of his Merry Men, I could call him by just his first name.)
   I'm really glad to be a Merry Man. I've asked my parents for a bow and arrows for my birthday. If I get them, I'll learn how to shoot as soon as I can. Maybe you could tell me the best kind to get.
   Anyway, why I'm writing is I want to know when I can come to Sherwood Forest and share

113

your adventures. Please let me know. If you're too busy to write, you can call me at 718 555-6923.

Thank you.

Sincerely,
Elizabeth Ann Silver

P.S. If somebody has a big harp, maybe I can play you a song.

I couldn't wait to hear from him again. Once he had told me when would be a good time to go to Sherwood Forest, I'd figure out how to get there. Maybe Buster would be willing to go again, or Tessa's mom. Or maybe even my parents—except I wasn't sure I wanted them around when I met him. My mom would get upset at the weapons and my dad would probably make some silly jokes.

Anyway, I thought my letter was a pretty good one, even though I was a little nervous about the harp part. I had to be able to play a real song soon. I had to be. But I didn't know about playing it for a bunch of people like the Merry Men. Maybe I'd ask Allan-a-Dale for tips on overcoming stage fright.

Anyway, like I said, things were definitely looking up—until Sunday at six P.M. Rona had a date with Toby. But before it she asked me to quiz her on my Robin Hood book, which she'd finished reading. I made up the quiz and everything, and I was proud of it.

114

"Okay," I said. "One: What was Robin Hood's title before he became an outlaw?"

"The Earl of Huntington," Rona answered promptly.

"Good. Two: Who was King Richard's mother?"

"Queen Eleanor."

"Right. You're doing good, Rona. Three: King Richard went off to fight in . . .?"

"The Crusades. That was an easy one," she said, looking a little smug.

"Okay then, how about this. Four: What false name did Little John use when he beat the Sheriff of Nottingham in a bout at Nottingham Faire?"

Rona frowned. I could see she was thinking hard. Finally, she said, "Robert Oaktree."

"Wrong. Reynold Greenleaf."

"That was too hard, Lizzie."

"No it wasn't. You have to pay more attention. . . . Okay, here's the last one. Five: What is deer meat called?"

Rona smiled broadly. "Venison. . . . Now, I've got one for you, Lizzie. How did Robin Hood die?"

I stared at her. "Robin Hood didn't die. I mean, he was a real person, so he must've died, but he doesn't die in any of his books."

"That's what you think. He does too die. You just don't have any of the books where he does. But Toby read some, and he told me about them. He saw it on TV too. On TV, nasty Guy of Gisborne's nasty sister poisoned Robin Hood because Robin killed her brother."

"Ugh!" I said, clapping my hands over my ears.

"I'm surprised you think that's so disgusting—it's what Ariadne does to those crickets you feed her. Poisons them, then sucks out their juices." Rona's eyes were shining wickedly.

I knew she was getting back at me for all the times I'd fed Ariadne in front of her. "I don't believe you. Robin doesn't die—especially like that."

"You can ask Toby next time if you don't believe me."

I didn't answer her.

She got up off my bed. "Anyway, thanks for helping me," she said.

I was still mad at her, though, so I didn't say, "You're welcome."

Suddenly she stopped grinning. "Hey, they're only stories anyway. Toby says there are so many different Robin Hood stories because people told them to each other instead of writing them down. In fact, he says, in another story Robin's cousin made him bleed to death—"

"Stop it!" I yelled. "Robin Hood didn't get poisoned or bleed to death. If he died—when he died—it was in a fair fight or something. And I don't want to hear anything else about how he died anyway. It's . . . it's . . . *mordred*."

Rona began to laugh. "You mean *morbid*, dummy," she said.

116

"Get out of here, Rona," I said.

She went, still laughing.

I should have known right then and there that things were about to take a turn for the worse. But I didn't want to think morbid thoughts.

It was on Wednesday that it happened. But there were signs on Monday and Tuesday, if I'd known how to read them.

On Monday Ms. Bronson sat in at my harp lesson, smiling and nodding the whole time. I didn't know why she was there, but she made me nervous and I kept messing up my fingering. Mr. Jasper didn't seem to notice her, though—he was just as mean as ever. He even made me tune a string. He hit a tuning fork and said, "Now, that string should exactly match the note this fork plays." I couldn't understand what he was talking about. I used the tuning key and turned the peg like he showed me, but when I plucked the string, both he and Ms. Bronson made faces. Finally Mr. Jasper tuned it himself.

Later that day, when I went to Markham's, Lavinia the dove was looking a little sick. She didn't make any noise when I came in, and she didn't seem hungry. I left a note for Markham and went home, a little worried.

Tuesday Tessa and I went to the beach. It was nice and peaceful there, and we were having a really good

117

time when all of a sudden who should turn up but Julie Lindstrom with a bunch of other girls.

"Uh-oh," said Tessa. "I probably shouldn't have mentioned her name last week. I summoned the devil."

Julie didn't say hello to us, but she sat nearby with her friends. They laughed and fooled around a lot, and Julie laughed loudest of all. It was like she wanted us to see how much fun she was having and we weren't, or something silly like that. I knew if we got up and moved, she'd take credit for that somehow, too, but it was better than having to hear her laughing away all afternoon.

So we moved. After a while we got thirsty, and I went to get us sodas. And who should be right in front of me at the refreshment stand? Julie Lindstrom, of course.

This time she couldn't pretend she didn't see me, because she turned around and bumped me with her cardboard soda tray. "Oh, I'm sor—" she began and stopped. "Oh, hello, Lizzie," she said coolly.

"Hello, Julie. Having a good summer?"

"Very good," she said. "And you?"

"Very good." I nodded.

Then I saw this little expression come over her face. It was one I'd seen before and hoped I wouldn't see again.

"Are you here with Tessa?" she asked, even though she knew I was.

"Yes."

"Oh, that's nice. I guess you're going to miss her when she goes to Pemborough."

"She's not going," I said, instantly realizing my mistake.

"She's not? She's going to give up the scholarship and everything?"

"She . . . uh . . . she hasn't decided yet," I said, trying to patch up what I'd done.

"Well, she better decide soon. She has less than three weeks."

I almost blurted out, "Don't remind me, you creep." But instead, I said, as casually as I could, "I'm sure she will."

Julie smiled a sickening smile at me.

"How come you know so much about Tessa and Pemborough?" I asked.

"My aunt is a teacher there. She told my mother somebody from my school was accepted there. . . . Try to have a good summer, Lizzie," she answered, and left.

As I walked back to Tessa, I hoped Julie's aunt was a lot nicer than her niece, or I wouldn't last at Pemborough more than a week.

The rest of our afternoon at the beach was fine. But when I went to Markham's later, Lavinia looked worse and my note to him was still in the same place. He must be out of town, I thought. He hadn't said anything

120

about going, but he doesn't always tell me his plans. I wondered if I should take Lavinia to a vet. I finally decided if she wasn't better the next day, I'd do that.

The next day was Wednesday. In the morning I had the best Robin Hood dream yet. We climbed a tree. We were high up and we could see for miles—forests and fields and hills. It was beautiful. Robin looked just the way he did at the Medieval Faire. "Someday this will be mine again, to roam free, far and wide," he said.

"We will roam together," said I.

"Yes. Together."

I woke up with a big smile on my face.

I didn't know my dream was the calm before the storm.

I got to my harp lesson a few minutes early, so I thought I'd practice. Nobody was in the room. I sat down and leaned the harp into position, but before I started to play it, I heard voices outside the room.

"The child has no talent," I heard Mr. Jasper say. I could recognize his voice anywhere.

"That's an exaggeration, Karl." That one was Ms. Bronson.

"Oh, perhaps she has a sense of rhythm, but she has no talent," he repeated.

"We are not in the business of turning away students," Ms. Bronson said, "simply because they do not meet your standards of—"

"And what of your standards, Beryl? You heard her."

There was a pause, and then I heard Beryl say, "I admit she seems to lack a certain aptitude, but she has only been studying for a short time."

There was another pause. I wondered who they were talking about, but it was probably nobody I knew anyway, since I hardly knew anybody at the school. Then the door opened. Mr. Jasper and Ms. Bronson walked in. When they saw me, Mr. Jasper merely nodded, but Ms. Bronson said in a startled voice, "Oh, Miss Silver. Aren't you early?"

"I guess so. Just a little."

She smiled. "Practicing, I see. How determined you are. Well, I'll leave you to your lesson now."

Throughout the lesson Mr. Jasper seemed different. He didn't yell at me or say anything nasty for a change. And I was glad about that. But he didn't seem to be quite so . . . *interested* in what I was doing either. He just had me play "Mary Had a Little Lamb" and didn't say much else.

Finally, at the end of the lesson, I asked, "Mr. Jasper, how am I doing? Will I be able to play a real song soon? I don't want to be pushy, but you see—"

"Sit down, Miss Silver," Mr. Jasper interrupted in a weary voice.

"I am sitting, Mr. Jasper."

"Oh . . . yes. Miss Silver, the time has come to be frank."

"Frank, Mr. Jasper?"

"Yes. I drove you hard, Miss Silver, as I drive all my students, because you expressed a desire to learn the harp. I believe one must play it—indeed any instrument—well or not at all. Perhaps I seemed too harsh to you." He paused.

"No, you didn't," I lied.

"At any rate, I have appraised your abilities carefully over the past several weeks, and I feel I must tell you you are wasting your money and your time, Miss Silver. You do not have any aptitude for the harp."

I stared at him a full minute without speaking. When I finally did, my voice was all squeaky and small. "You want me to quit, Mr. Jasper?"

"I strongly advise it, Miss Silver."

I stood up in a fog and walked toward the door. Somewhere in that fog I realized it was me he and Ms. Bronson had been talking about. Me. Miss No-Talent Silver.

"Although she will balk, you may ask for a refund for Friday's lesson from Ms. Bronson," Mr. Jasper was saying.

I reached the door and turned. "Mr. Jasper," I said in the same squeaky voice, "what instrument do I have talent for?"

Mr. Jasper thought a minute. "I would suggest you return to the claves, Miss Silver."

I nodded and slowly walked out of the room, down

123

the hall and into the street.

It wasn't until I was halfway home that I decided I didn't want to go there.

So I went to Markham's instead. I was still in a fog while I fed the rabbits and Little Flower. I got to the doves' cage, opened it to put in food and only then noticed Lavinia wasn't there.

"Oh no," I moaned. "Lavinia. Poor Lavinia." And then I sank down into a chair and started to cry.

16

My parents didn't think I could hear them whispering, but I could.

"Something's definitely wrong with Lizzie," my mother was saying. "She was doing so well, being so responsible, and all of a sudden, poof. She stopped her harp lessons. She asked me to call Markham and say she couldn't work for him anymore. She's refused to see Tessa for five days. I asked her if anyone had hurt her, and she said no. I'm certain she was telling the truth. So what's going on?"

"Growing pains, maybe," Dad said.

"I don't know. . . . Why do you think she stopped those lessons, David?"

"She said she didn't like the harp," my dad told her.

"I'm not sure I believe that."

"Have you talked to her?"

"I've tried. She hardly says anything. She's drooping, David, and frankly I'm worried."

"I think we should let her alone. If she doesn't snap out of it in a while, I'll talk to her, okay?"

"I guess so. . . . But I just can't understand it."

I heard Mom walking out of the kitchen, and I quietly walked up the stairs where I'd been sitting and back to my room.

What my parents didn't understand was that I'd given up. I had two weeks left before Tessa told Pemborough she was coming. And two weeks wasn't enough time to learn anything. Especially for a no-talent like me.

Even Robin Hood had given up on me. I hadn't gotten an answer to my letter. And the last dream I'd had about him was rotten. I was sitting by the fire with Robin and all the Merry Men.

"Play something for us, Elizabeth," said Robin.

"Aye," said Little John. "Play us a merry tune."

The other men chimed in. "Aye, a dancing air." "Hurrah for minstrel Elizabeth." "She has harpist's hands."

Someone handed me a harp, a small one just like Allan-a-Dale's.

I took it into my arms, smiled at my friends and began to play. But the sound that came out was awful. It sounded the way a piano does if you play all the keys at once.

The men groaned.

I tried it again and made the same noise.

The Merry Men began to grumble. "She has hands like dead fish," one of them said.

I looked down, and instead of hands, I had two fish. They stared at me with dead eyes.

I yelled and woke up.

Fortunately, I didn't wake anybody else up.

That was last night. Now I said to Ariadne, "Do you know how lucky you are to be a spider? You have plenty of talent. You spin silk and always look beautiful. And your best friend will never leave you."

Ariadne shuffled into a corner of her cage.

Downstairs, the phone rang. Dad answered it. "Lizzie, it's for you," he called.

"I'm busy," I called back.

There was a pause, and Dad said, "It's Buster, and he says it's important."

I sighed. Even though I didn't want to talk to anybody, I thought it would be rude not to answer—especially since it was Buster, whom I hadn't spoken to in a week, and because he said it was important. He's like Tessa—he never says something's important unless it is. I only hoped his important news wasn't like hers.

I went to the phone. Dad politely left the room. "Hi, Buster," I said.

"Hello, Gloriana. I went to Markham's today hoping

to speak to you, but he told me you were taking a leave of absence."

I didn't say anything.

"He thought it was because you blamed yourself for Lavinia's problem."

I thought about that a minute. Did I blame myself that she had died? I didn't think so. "No, I don't," I told Buster. "But I miss her."

"You can come and see her anytime," Buster said.

"What? You mean she's okay? She didn't die?"

"Oh, no, not at all. Markham found your note and took Lavinia straight to the vet. I guess you must've come to feed her while she was gone. The vet said Lavinia wanted to lay an egg, but the egg was stuck. He administered a bit of olive oil, and out it came."

"Lavinia laid an egg?"

"Doves sometimes do, even without mates."

"Wow!" It was the first good thing that had happened in a long time.

"So perhaps you'll end your leave of absence. The animals miss you, and so does Markham."

I sighed. "I don't know, Buster. . . ."

"Is something else the matter, Gloriana?"

I thought a minute, and then I said, "Remember what you told me—about a man's reach exceeding his grasp?"

"Yes."

"Well, I guess my arm's just too short."

"What do you mean, Lizzie?" he asked.

And I told him.

When I finished, Buster said, "Good breeding forbids me from telling you what sort of a person your teacher is."

"Well, Mr. Jasper may be a creep, but he isn't dumb. I *don't* have any musical talent, Buster. I never will."

"Nonsense. *Everyone* has musical talent. I have a friend who can prove that to you. In fact, I thought perhaps you'd like to meet him this coming weekend."

"Where?"

"Ah, I will reveal that in a moment. But first, answer one question. Have you had the chicken pox?"

"Yes. When I was seven."

"Excellent. Then I see no problem."

"No problem in what?"

"In your going to the Medieval Faire this coming weekend."

"The Medieval Faire!"

"Yes. That's my important news, Lizzie. I've been hired to work there—as a wandering poet and occasional minstrel. In fact, that's where I was this past weekend."

"Buster, how wonderful!"

"Wait, Gloriana. There's more. The people who run the fair asked me if I know a boy or girl aged ten or eleven who's had the chicken pox and could work at the fair this weekend. It seems they're a bit short

129

staffed due to an outbreak of chicken pox. I said I thought I knew just the right person."

"Do you mean me?" I squealed. "Tessa hasn't had chicken pox. But I have."

"I do indeed. Are you interested?"

"Am I?" I yelled. "You bet! I'll ask Mom and Dad right now."

"Wait a minute, Lizzie. Tell them you'll be working from Friday through Sunday, and that the Frobish family will be putting us up. Andy Frobish is a performer at the fair, and he and his mother own a summer house near it. We will leave at six A.M. on Friday to get you there on time for a costume fitting and instructions, and we'll get home at about nine or ten on Sunday night."

"Wow!" I yelled again, and rushed off to tell my folks. Mom insisted upon getting on the phone and hearing straight from Buster the same thing I'd just told her. Then she said I could go.

I grabbed the phone back from her. "I love you, Buster," I yelled.

"I love you, too, Gloriana. I'll speak with you tomorrow so we can brush up on our British accents together. Cheerio."

I hung up and began to dance around the room. "Hear ye, hear ye," I announced. "Elizabeth Silver is going to join Robin Hood at Sherwood Forest in only four days. And she can hardly wait!"

17

For the next three days all I could think about was meeting Robin Hood. What would I say when I met him? What would he say? Would I help him in any of his adventures?

When I told Tessa about the whole thing, she got excited too—after she stopped being mad at me for not talking to her for so long. I explained that I'd had some problems, but I didn't tell her what they were. My problems were the last thing I wanted to talk about.

"Do you think he'll remember me?" I asked her. "Do you think he'll like me? Do you—"

"Lizzie, stop worrying. He'll like you fine. I like you and I've got very good taste," said Tessa.

That made me laugh and feel better for a while. But pretty soon I started thinking about Robin again, and

I felt all nervous and excited once more.

I also kept wondering what my job was going to be at the fair. Buster didn't know. He said the people who organized it would tell me the day we arrived. I thought about the people I'd seen there—singing, dancing, juggling, playing instruments. I couldn't do any of those things. I could do a cartwheel, though, like that funny red-haired kid I dunked. Boy, I sure hoped it wasn't *his* job I had to take. I didn't feel like getting wet.

I wondered what my costume would look like, too, but Buster didn't know that either. I hoped it would be green like Robin's, but brown like what some of the Merry Men wore would be okay, too. I didn't want to wear a diamond-patterned suit like the Artful Dodger's, and as for a dress, that was at the bottom of my list.

Finally, Thursday night came. I was lying in bed wide awake. I had to wake up at five o'clock the next morning, and I knew I should get some sleep, but I just couldn't. I kept seeing Robin—the way he'd bravely fought Little John and the way he'd winked at me and told me I could be a Merry Man. I got up, took out his letter and read it for the millionth time. I wondered for a minute why he hadn't answered my second letter, but then I thought, It doesn't matter; I'm going to meet him tomorrow and I can ask him myself. That got me so excited all over again that I gave up trying to sleep and took one of my Robin Hood books out of my backpack. I read for about an hour and then I closed my eyes.

"I shall win that archery contest," Robin said as we approached Nottingham Faire.

"A marksman monk? The king and queen will be surprised," I said.

"So will the Sheriff of Nottingham."

"Oh, Robin, take care."

"I'll leave that to you, my gentle Elizabeth. For who would suspect a dainty damsel in a dress of being an outlaw's bodyguard?"

We grinned at each other.

The faire was bright with banners and people in gaily colored apparel selling their wares.

"There is quite a crowd over yonder. I wonder what is there," said Robin.

"I see . . . targets! The contest must be about to begin!"

"Then I must take my place among the contestants. You join the onlookers and keep your eyes open for the sheriff and his men."

"That I will," I said and went over to the waiting crowd.

I must've waited with them a long time because the next thing I knew, my alarm clock was ringing.

It was dark out and everybody was still asleep when I got up. I yawned a lot and had to stick my head under the faucet to stop. I didn't want to fall asleep at the fair and miss Robin. I made myself breakfast and waited outside with my backpack for Buster.

He was right on time. I got into the car, and he let

out a big yawn. "This is way past my bedtime," he said.

I laughed.

This time, on the ride to the fair, I did most of the talking. I chattered about Robin and the adventures I most liked and how excited I was and everything.

Buster smiled and yawned a lot and apologized for yawning and yawned some more.

"It's neat that those singers helped you get this job," I said. "Do you think you'll sell a lot of poems?"

"Well, if I sell three or four, that'll be three or four more than I've sold before."

"I bet you'll sell more than that," I said.

"That's why I like you, Gloriana. You're an optimist."

"So are you," I said.

"I know. Aren't we splendid?"

We both giggled.

Then we arrived at the fair. We went to what Buster said was the administration building. There was a woman waiting for us. "Hello, Clovis. Is this Elizabeth Silver? Good, come this way."

She took me to a room and said, "Elizabeth, here's your costume. Try it on and we'll see if it has to be altered." She held it out to me.

It was a long pink skirt and a fluffy white blouse. Tessa would've loved it.

"Pretty, isn't it?" the woman said.

I nodded politely, thinking the whole time, "How's Robin going to recognize me in this?" I went into a dressing room and tried on the dress. It fit all right. I came out, and Buster said, "Ravishing, Gloriana."

"Let's get you some makeup," the woman said.

"Makeup?"

"Uh-huh." She took me to another room, where there was a table with a mirror, and sat me down in a chair and put lipstick, eyeliner and powder on me.

I looked at myself in the mirror, and I could hardly recognize myself.

"What's my job here?" I asked her.

"Mr. Trelane will tell you. He'll be with you soon." She checked out my face and frowned. I thought she was noticing my buck teeth, but she said, "What should we do with your hair? It's at an in-between length."

"Give her a hat, Carney," a man said. I could see him in the mirror. He was almost as big as Little John. He came over to me. "You're one of our replacements, right?"

I nodded.

"Keep your head still," the woman called Carney said. "I'm just going to touch up your left eye."

"While you're keeping your head still, keep your ears open," said the big man, who must've been Mr. Trelane. "Here are your assignments for the weekend." He spoke very quickly, as though he was in a big hurry.

135

I felt my heart give a bump. Robin Hood. Put me with Robin Hood, I prayed.

While Carney got a big straw hat, put it on my head and tied a big bow under my chin, Mr. Trelane said, "From eleven to twelve-thirty you will hand out flowers at Posy Bridge. Get there at ten-forty-five. From twelve-thirty to one-thirty you'll have lunch. From one-thirty to three you'll help at the Tilting Booth. After a half-hour break you'll return to Posy Bridge until five o'clock, when you will join in the Grand Parade to the grounds of Shining Castle. Got that? Here's a copy of the schedule in case you forget." He left before I could ask him a single question.

"Wait . . . Mr. Trelane . . . wait a minute . . ."

"He's busy, honey," said the woman. "There. You're finished." She started to leave, too.

"Wait, Carney . . . I mean, Ms. Carney . . . uh . . ."

"It's just Carney. Short for Carnation," she said, pausing near the door. "What do you want, sweetie?"

"I . . . I want to know where do I get the flowers? Do I have any lines to say? Is the Tilting Booth that ride where the wooden horse slides down a rope? What do I do there? And what do I do in the Grand Parade?" I said as fast as possible before she left, too.

"Here are the flowers. No, you don't have any lines as far as I know, but you're free to write your own. Yes, the Tilting Booth is that ride for little kids—the man who runs it will tell you what to do. And in the

137

Grand Parade, you march." She looked out the door. "Oh, no. What did you do to your hair?" she said to someone, and hurried out.

My head was whirling a little when I left the room. I was glad Mr. Trelane had given me the schedule, because I wasn't sure I could remember everything he told me. I realized I'd better get a map, too, because the fair was big and I didn't remember where Posy Bridge or the Tilting Booth were. My mind was so busy, I bumped right into somebody and blinked. It was the Artful Dodger.

He stared at me for a minute. "You look familiar." He snapped his fingers. "Why, if it isn't Elizabeth Silver of Sherwood Forest, in disguise, no doubt. Is it not?"

I blinked again. He was waiting for a reply. I recovered quickly. "Yes, it is. And you'd better watch out!"

"Oh, I will. I will," he said with a grin. Then he pulled my hat over my eyes.

"Why, you . . ." I said, fumbling with my hat. When I got it fixed, the Artful Dodger was gone. But Buster was coming out of a room, with a pole and a banner saying "POEMS."

"Ready, Gloriana?" he asked.

I took a deep breath. "Ready as I'll ever be."

"Good. I'll escort you to Posy Bridge, then pick you up for lunch."

We left the building. I saw a lot of people opening booths or taking their positions on the grounds. I kept my eyes open for Robin Hood or his Merry Men, but I didn't see any of them.

When we got to the bridge, Buster said, "You're on your own now, Lizzie. Just don't forget to smile."

"I won't," I said.

Buster strolled away and I realized I was here, really here. And Robin was lurking somewhere nearby. Maybe just behind that tree. My heart gave another bump, and I started to smile for all I was worth.

18

I heard about a weird disease where your mouth gets locked in one position and you can't move it. I wondered if I'd gotten that disease, because my mouth felt stuck. But it was probably just from smiling nonstop for an hour and a half.

Lots of people had come by. I smiled at all of them and gave each one a flower. I didn't talk much to anybody and nobody much talked to me either, except for one little kid who wanted my hat and started howling when his mother said he couldn't have it. And I didn't see Robin Hood at all.

At twelve-thirty on the dot, a girl in a blue skirt and a white blouse appeared, carrying a flower basket. "Hi, I'm here to take your place," she said.

I stepped off the bridge and massaged my mouth.

Then Buster arrived and we went to lunch. I asked him if he'd sold any poems.

"One and one half," he answered.

"One half of a poem?"

"Yes. The customer liked only the first verse."

We both laughed at that.

After lunch I went to the Tilting Booth. It was this really neat ride. A little kid would climb up a ladder to a platform and get on a wooden horse. The man who ran the ride would hand the kid a lance, which is a long pole like a huge blunt sword with a hilt, and a shield. Then the horse would slide down a pulley rope and stop at a stuffed dummy of a knight. My job, it turned out, was to help the kids off the horse when the ride ended.

At least I don't have to smile the whole time, I thought, taking my place.

But after forty-five minutes of lifting chunky little kids off the horse, my arms and back started to ache. And I had forty-five more minutes to go.

Tony, the man who ran the ride, said to take a five-minute break. I went over to a patch of grass, took off my hat and stretched out with my eyes closed. It felt good to lie down—even though I knew it was for just a short time. All of a sudden something wet and cold plopped right on my nose. I opened my eyes with a start. The Artful Dodger was grinning down at me, a dripping ice-cream cone in his hand.

"Tsk, tsk," he said. "I thought Elizabeth Silver of Sherwood Forest would know better than to leave herself open to attack."

I moved my foot and tripped him. His ice cream cone flew out of his hand and landed in a nearby bush.

I sprang up. "Elizabeth Silver never leaves herself open to attack," I said.

But the Artful Dodger wasn't listening. He was staring mournfully at his ice cream cone. " 'Alf a crown that cost me," he said. "I'm just a poor lad. I can't be affordin' treats all the time."

"You should have thought of that before you . . ." I fumbled in my mind for the right words from one of my Robin Hood books. And I found them. "Before you set upon me," I finished.

But he looked so miserable, I fished around in the pocket of my skirt and found two of the four quarters I'd stuck there just in case I needed them. "Here. Let it never be said Elizabeth Silver of Sherwood Forest does not help the poor."

The Artful Dodger took the quarters and began to smile again. Slowly, he took something off his belt. It was a leather purse, and it was bulging. He dropped the two quarters into it and shook the purse up and down. It was so full of coins, it barely jingled.

"Why you . . ." I began.

But the Artful Dodger laughed and ran off before I could finish.

142

I shook my head, but I had to laugh, too. That kid was something else. Then I went back to work.

It was two-fifty-five. I had only five minutes left to work at the Tilting Booth. Then I could take a half-hour break before I had to go smile for another hour and a half at Posy Bridge. I still hadn't seen Robin, and I was beginning to wonder if I'd make it through the day, when suddenly a commotion made me turn my head. All around me people stopped what they were doing to watch.

Someone was running through the trees in front of me. Someone in Lincoln green. And he was being chased by two men all in black. "There goes the fiend!" one of the men in black shouted.

"Catch that outlaw or the sheriff will have our hides," cried the other.

"It's him!" I yelled. "Robin! Robin Hood!" I took a step away from the booth.

But the men had disappeared, and the next thing I knew, a little kid was sitting on the ground, crying.

"Oh, no, is he all right?" I said.

His mother rushed over and checked the boy out. "He's all right. No thanks to you," she said, snatching him up and stomping angrily away.

Tony scolded me, too. "You're supposed to watch these kids. If they get hurt, this whole fair could get sued."

143

"I'm sorry. It won't happen again."

"It better not. . . . Now go take your break."

I went, gladly. I hurried off in the direction I'd seen Robin go. But I didn't see him again. I got myself a cup of apple juice with my last two quarters and drank it thirstily. It made me feel better. The Parade, I thought. If I don't see him before then, I'm sure to see him in the Parade. I went smiling to Posy Bridge.

My time there was pretty much the same as it had been in the morning, except that Buster came by a couple of times—once singing with the other troubadours.

I was almost out of flowers when I heard a fanfare of horns.

"The Parade!" I yelled. "Hooray!"

I stood by the path that wove through the trees, around the fair. Pretty soon the horn players came into view. Behind them marched people from the fair in all their fancy costumes. Darting in and out among the marchers, turning cartwheels, was none other than the Artful Dodger. He flipped to his feet, saw me and exclaimed, "Come, Elizabeth. Come join the Parade."

Clutching my basket, I skipped to the end of the line. I kept looking this way and that for Robin Hood as we marched to Shining Castle. I followed the marchers up the steps and down again until we came to a big green. A low fence surrounded the whole area. We marchers were inside it. On the other side was a big

144

crowd; some people were sitting, others were standing. I sat down with the other marchers and waited. I didn't know what we were waiting for. Buster, Tessa and I hadn't stayed at the fair long enough to see this part of it.

Suddenly a cheer went up, and a coach drawn by four white horses appeared. A man and woman each wearing a crown stepped from it.

"All hail the king and queen!" a big woman next to me yelled.

"All hail!" I yelled with everyone else.

I couldn't believe what was happening. It was like a play and real life all mixed together.

The king made a speech. Next someone he called the bishop blessed the proceedings. Then we waited a bit longer until four men came out onto the green. They were carrying big round things. They set them up on stands.

"Targets!" I said out loud. "They're setting up targets!"

"Hooray for the archery contest!" the woman next to me called.

My brain whirled. It was just like my dream.

A page came out and announced, "The first two contestants are Eric of Durham and Geront Collier."

Two men came out and drew their bows. Eric of Durham hit the white ring on the edge of the target, but Geront Collier's arrow missed altogether.

Everyone clapped politely.

Two more contestants came out and tried. They did a little better. One hit the black ring, which is inside the white, and the other hit the blue, which is inside the black. The closer to the bull's-eye you hit, the better you score.

We clapped again.

Then the final two marksmen came out. One was all in black. The other was dressed in a brown monk's robe.

"The Sheriff of Nottingham and Friar Sparrow," the page announced.

Friar Sparrow turned to where I was sitting and pushed aside his hood.

I gasped. It was Robin!

The sheriff shot first. He hit the red ring—only two rings away from a bull's-eye. Then Robin shot. He hit the red ring too.

"Hooray for Friar Sparrow," the woman next to me called out.

"Hooray!" shouted several other people.

"These are the best marksmen. They will have two more chances to break their tie," said the queen.

The page stepped forward. "Second shot."

The sheriff fitted the notch of his arrow to the bowstring. He drew and released.

"Gold ring! Nine points!" said the page. "Friar Sparrow."

"Friar Sparrow" barely looked at the target. He let

fly an arrow. It too struck the gold ring.

The crowd cheered.

"Final shot," the page announced.

The sheriff faced the target. He stood still for a long time, concentrating deeply. He took careful aim.

Thwack! Bull's-eye!

The sheriff smiled a greasy smile at the crowd. Everyone booed.

"Well, Friar. Let us see you beat that," he said.

Robin stepped up to the shooting line. He stood, concentrating, just as the sheriff had. He raised his bow. "Now!" he cried. He spun his body in the direction of the other target. His bowstring twanged. And before anyone could wink, Robin's arrow had split the sheriff's neatly down the middle.

The crowd gasped, then roared.

Above them, the sheriff's voice rose. "There is but one in all Nottinghamshire who can shoot like that. And that one is . . ." His hand went to the sword on his belt.

"Look out, Friar Sparrow!" the woman next to me called.

"Robin Hood!" said the sheriff.

And I leaped to my feet. "Robin, look out!" I yelled. I jumped over the legs of the person in front of me and, seizing a sword from the belt of a nearby soldier, I charged onto the green. "Flee, Robin, flee!" I cried. "I'll hold him off."

Both Robin and the sheriff stood there unmoving.

"Know you not your bodyguard, Elizabeth Silver?" I said. "Hurry!"

All of a sudden the sheriff gave a little shake of his head and lunged for me. I waved my sword at him. He backed away. "Run, Robin!" I hollered.

"Men!" the sheriff bellowed.

Two men in black edged toward me on the green. I waved my sword at them. They backed off.

"What's going on here?" one of them said.

Robin was still standing still. Then, from the corner of my eye, I saw him give a little shake, too. He threw off the monk's robe and reached to pluck a sword out of a soldier's belt. But there was no sword. I'd already taken it.

"Get the girl!" the sheriff was yelling.

"You'll never take me alive!" I said.

"Give me thy sword and flee," Robin said to me.

"Never. Your life is worth more than—" I never finished my sentence, because somebody had grabbed me from behind. The sword flew out of my hand. The sheriff picked it up and tossed it to Robin.

"Huh?" I said.

The sheriff and Robin began to fight. But one of the sheriff's men crept up behind Robin.

"No! Robin, look out!" I screamed.

Robin spun around and bumped into the man. He went sprawling.

"Jeez," I heard the sheriff swear under his breath.

"What are we going to do?"

"Get that kid out of here," Robin said. "And ad-lib."

The next thing I knew, whoever was holding me had dragged me off the green and behind the castle.

"If I let you go, will you promise not to run out there again?" my captor said.

"Yes," I whispered.

He released me, and I finally saw him. He was one of the sheriff's men. He was also Tony from the Tilting Booth. "You?" he said when he realized who I was.

I gulped. All of a sudden it was like somebody'd taken a hood off my head. I sat down on the ground. I stayed like that for a few minutes until I heard an angry voice say, "Okay, where is she? Where's that crazy kid?" Robin Hood charged over, grabbed me by the shoulders, pulled me up and began to shake me. "You bozo. You jerk. Just what do you think you were doing? That fight was carefully planned. You wrecked it. It's a miracle nobody got hurt. Who hired you anyway? You're a menace. Somebody should call your agent and make sure you don't work in this business again." He stopped shaking me. "Where's Trelane?" he said to Tony. "I want her barred from this place permanently." He turned to me again. "Did you hear me? I want you barred. Show your face here again and you'll get a lesson from Byron Lord you'll never forget." He gave me another shake and stalked off.

I gulped again. Tears started to trickle down my cheeks. I turned my head. The Artful Dodger was standing there. He'd probably seen the whole thing.

He handed me a handkerchief. "Don't mind him," he said. "He's just angry because you upstaged him. I thought you were great!"

"Oh, shut up!" I yelled, and shoving him aside, I ran all the way to the administration building.

19

"Gloriana, are you in there?" Buster's voice called softly.

I blinked. My hand brushed against some cloth and I sneezed. I wiped my nose and blinked again. It took me a minute to realize I was sitting in the dark on the floor of the costume room and another minute to remember how I'd gotten there. But I had no idea how long I'd actually been there.

"Gloriana?" Buster called again.

I guess I was in shock. What had I done? I mean, how could I have done what I'd done? I'd gotten carried away once before, but that was okay. I mean, it was sort of fun and Robin had liked it. . . . But this time! This time I really messed up. I was done for. I'd failed at the harp. I was going to lose Tessa. And now I'd made Robin Hood mad at me, too. Except he wasn't Robin. That's where I'd really gone wrong. He was an actor, just an actor. I'd known that all along. But somehow I'd believed he wasn't.

The door opened. The light went on. Buster picked up the hems of some dresses and peered at me. "There you are." He sat down next to me.

I felt myself about to cry again.

"I can see why you chose this room. It is comfortable. A bit stuffy, but comfortable nevertheless."

I didn't say anything.

"Should we bring our dinner in here? I can order out—"

"Buster," I said, "I think you better take me right to a hospital."

"A hospital? Are you hurt?" he said, serious and concerned.

"No. I need to see a psychiatrist. I'm crazy."

Buster put his hand under my chin and looked at me. "You're not crazy, Lizzie. You're . . . imaginative. Like me."

"Imaginative? You call messing up a play and getting everybody mad at me imaginative?" I said.

"You didn't mess up the play. The audience loved it. I'm afraid you did upset a few of the actors. But they'll get over it."

"Oh, Buster, don't try to make me feel better. I really blew it this time."

We were quiet for a minute. Then Buster said, "If anyone's to blame, I am."

"You? How?"

153

"I gave you the Robin Hood books. I brought you to the fair. And perhaps I encouraged you to believe in Robin Hood a little too much."

I shook my head. "Uh-uh. I did that all by myself."

We were quiet again.

Then I said, "Buster, how come what a person makes up in her head is more fun than what's real?"

Buster was quiet for a moment. "I don't know," he finally said. "But it's also true that sometimes what's real can be more fun than what you make up. Like the magic show you were in—where you got Ariadne. Or like Ariadne herself. Didn't you once tell me you were more interested in real animals than in imaginary ones?"

I gave him a sheepish look. "That's true. I did. I like science, too, because it's about what's real—"

"But it's also about what we imagine. The best scientists have feet in both worlds."

I sighed. "I think one of my feet slipped."

Buster laughed. I had to, too.

"Well," he said, "shall we go to the Frobishes'? They're expecting us."

"I guess so." I stood up, shook my stiff legs and went to change my clothes.

It was still light out as we drove to the Frobishes'. Buster said they lived about half an hour from the fair.

I didn't talk much during the ride. I was feeling kind of embarrassed.

155

Buster had said that Andy Frobish worked at the fair. If he had seen my "act," he probably wouldn't want to have anything to do with me. He certainly wouldn't want me staying over in his house, even for the night. But I didn't have much choice. Buster couldn't drive me all the way home and then come back himself so he could work the next day. And it was too late for me to take a bus alone—even if my mom allowed it, which she wouldn't. No, I'd just have to leave tomorrow— because I sure wasn't going back to the fair—and spend the night at the Frobishes', even if Andy couldn't stand me.

We turned down a narrow road with trees on either side. "The Frobishes live in the woods?" I asked.

"In the summer. During the rest of the year, I believe they live in Brooklyn—not too far from you, as a matter of fact."

We pulled into a pebbled driveway and up a slope to a lovely house made of red wood. "It's beautiful!" I said.

"Lots of good spiders around here," said Buster.

We got out of the car and climbed the steps to the porch. Buster knocked on the door.

"Come in," a voice sang out.

We went. Right into the living room. It was cozy, with a fireplace and spiral staircase right in the middle. "Look at that!" I pointed at it. Then a pretty woman with red hair entered. "Hello, Buster." She turned to me. "And this must be Lizzie."

I nodded.

"Ma, have you seen my . . ." A red-haired boy came flying into the room and skidded to a stop. He stared at me. I stared back. Then his face broke into a shy smile. "Hello, Elizabeth Silver," he said softly.

It took me a minute to speak. Finally, I said, "You? You're Andy Frobish?"

"Yes." His voice was different. I realized he'd lost his accent.

"You know each other?" Buster asked.

Andy and I nodded.

"How nice," said Andy's mother. "Andy, why don't you show Lizzie where she's going to sleep?"

"Okay," said Andy. He began to climb the staircase. I followed him slowly.

"Here's your room," he said, stopping at the second door in the hall.

"It's nice," I said.

"Do you want to see my room?"

I nodded. He was being so polite—not like the Artful Dodger at all. I guess that was just a character he played, like the actor playing Robin Hood, and not what he was really like.

Andy's room was next door, and it was incredible. He had posters of old-time movie stars, like Charlie Chaplin, and odd knickknacks like a cardboard crown and a hoop and a bracelet of bells. In the corner of

157

157

the room was a bunch of musical instruments—drums and cymbals and other things.

"What is this stuff?" I asked.

"Things from shows I've been in." He didn't say it in a bragging way.

"You've been acting a long time?" I asked.

"For about six years."

We didn't say anything for a minute. Then we both talked at once.

"I'm sorry I yelled at you before," I said.

"You know, I wasn't making fun of you before. I really thought you were great," said Andy.

We stopped, laughed, and tried it again—one at a time.

"Where did you study acting?" asked Andy.

"Nowhere. I'm not an actress."

"Yes you are," said Andy. "You've got a lot of talent."

"Me? You're crazy."

"I'm not crazy. I've worked with a lot of kids. I know who's good and who isn't. Anyway, if you're not an actress, how'd you get a job here?"

I told him the whole story. "So that's how," I finished.

"Amazing," he said. "You didn't even have to audition."

"No. But I don't think I was really supposed to do much acting either." I sighed. "I'll never go back there again."

"Sure you will. They need you. They really are short staffed. And as long as you don't ad-lib tomorrow, nobody'll even notice you."

"But Robin Hood . . . or whoever he is . . ."

"Byron Lord. That's his name. He won't do anything to you. He just has a big mouth."

"I don't know, Andy."

"Trust me," he said, in his Artful Dodger accent. "Andy Frobish never lies—at least, not while he's standing up. Barrum-bum." He stepped on a pedal, and the cymbals in the corner crashed.

"How come you have so many instruments?" I asked.

"Because I'm a one-boy band."

"A what?"

"Here . . . I'll show you." He picked up some cymbals and strapped them to the insides of his knees. He slipped something with strings and buttons on a strap over his shoulder. He called it an autoharp. He put a big drum with a pedal at one foot and the set of standing cymbals there, too. At the other foot he placed a tambourine. On a funny metal contraption that went around his neck, he put a kazoo.

"Pick a song. Any song," he said.

"Beethoven's Moonlight Sonata," I said. I remembered that because Tessa was working on it on the piano.

"Very funny."

"Okay. How about 'When the Saints Go Marchin' In'? I've always liked that one."

" 'When the Saints' it is."

Andy began to play his one-boy band. He blew his kazoo. He strummed his autoharp. He beat his drum, crashed his cymbals and rattled his tambourine. He was incredible.

When he finished, I applauded wildly. "That was great! How long did it take you to learn that?"

"About two days," he said.

"Two days! You must be a genius."

He laughed. "Anyone can learn it. Anyone who has a sense of rhythm."

All of a sudden, it was like my entire head lit up. A sense of rhythm. Mr. Jasper said I had a sense of rhythm. "Andy, do you . . . do you think . . . could you possibly . . . teach me?"

"Sure," he said. "Easy."

Tessa! I thought. Wait for me, Tessa. Just wait!

20

Andy was a much better teacher than Mr. Jasper. He was patient and encouraging. I told him why I had to learn to play the one-boy band. He didn't think it was strange. I asked him if I had to learn to read music to play it, and he laughed and said, "No way. I can't read a note myself."

He said "When the Saints Go Marching In" was a good choice, and he'd teach me to play that. First, he told me to hum the song into the kazoo. That was simple. Then he showed me how to play the song on the autoharp. I thought that would be difficult. The autoharp has all these strings and buttons. But it wasn't hard either. All I had to do was learn to press three buttons (one at a time) with one hand and strum the strings with the other.

161

"See, Lizzie, you're playing the harp after all," Andy said.

"This is more like a guitar than a harp," I said. But I was pleased just the same.

After I learned to strum the song, Andy made me do that and hum it into the kazoo at the same time. "Great!" he said. "Next, we add the percussion."

I said that sounded hard, but he told me not to worry. "You're a natural," he said. "You'll be able to play this in a couple of days."

I wanted to keep working on learning it that night, but Buster and Ms. Frobish made Andy and me go to bed.

The next day I woke up all tense. I didn't want to go to the fair and face Robin and Tony and Mr. Trelane. But Buster and Andy convinced me it would be okay and that if I needed any moral support, they'd be there.

Mr. Trelane greeted us as we arrived. He looked closely at me. "Elizabeth Silver?" he said.

I nodded, twitching under his stare.

"Today, you will not work—" he began.

"I understand, Mr. Trelane," I said, turning to go.

"At the Tilting Booth," he finished. "You're needed at the Maze instead to rescue any lost children. Are you familiar with the Maze?"

I turned back and nodded. Tessa and I had gone through it in two minutes. But while we were there, some little kids got lost and scared. We helped get them out.

"You will also work at Posy Bridge as you did yesterday," he said, and left quickly.

Andy, Buster and I looked at each other and shrugged. So much for worrying about Mr. Trelane or Tony of the Tilting Booth.

But Robin was another story. The day before I'd been hoping so much to meet him. Now I was hoping I wouldn't run into him.

And so, of course, I did.

It was while I was working my second shift at Posy Bridge. He came by with Maid Marian on his arm. I knew it was Maid Marian because he said, "Ah, Marian. There is much danger for you if we be seen together."

"I care not. There is naught they can do to me that is worse than tearing me from your side."

For a minute I wondered why they were playing this scene without an audience. There was nobody near the bridge to watch them.

But then both Robin and Marian laughed, and Marian said, "So, you want to go to Jason's with the crowd for dinner?"

Robin put his arms around her the way people do on those dumb soap operas my mom sometimes watches when she thinks nobody's around to notice. "No, let's go out alone tonight. Then we can go back to my

163

place, have some wine and demonstrate our affection for each other—"

"Shh," said Marian, looking over his shoulder at me. "A child."

Robin turned and saw me.

I gulped, ready for another bawling out.

But he just smiled. "Ah, the lovely flower girl. How about a posy for brave Robin Hood?"

He came over. I handed him a flower. "Thank thee, fair maiden," he said. He gave the flower to Marian.

As they walked away, I heard her say, "I wonder if that girl who tried to 'rescue' you yesterday is still working here."

"She better not be," said Robin. "I told Trelane to fire her, and Trelane always listens to me."

When they'd disappeared from view, I started to laugh. I kept laughing while I gave flowers to the next three people. They ended up laughing, too, even though they didn't know what was so funny.

The rest of the day was okay. I joined the parade and cheered at the archery contest and at the fight between Robin and the sheriff and at Robin's victory. And nobody said a thing to me. It was sort of fun, but to be honest, I was anxious to get back to the Frobishes' house and work on the one-boy band.

By ten o'clock on Saturday night I'd learned how to beat the bass drum, hit the cymbals and play the tambourine. But I hadn't learned how to put it all together with the kazoo and the autoharp. And Andy and I were both too tired to keep going.

"We need another day or two," he said.

"But we have to work at the fair again tomorrow, and then I have to go home," I said, panic rising in me.

"Why do you have to go home?"

"Because Buster's leaving tomorrow."

"Maybe he can stay an extra day. Let's go downstairs and ask."

We did. But Buster said he had to return to Brooklyn. He had things to do—especially concerning his Poem-In, which was the following week.

Andy and I went back upstairs. I sighed. "Well, thanks anyway, for teaching me. But I guess—"

"Oh, stop sounding so depressed, Lizzie. Where there's a will, there's a way." Then he called, "Hey, Mom, didn't you say you have to go back to the city this week for something?"

"Yes. I have a meeting with my editor on Tuesday," Ms. Frobish, who's a writer, answered from her room.

"Good. Can you drive Lizzie back to Brooklyn?"

"Sure," she answered.

"See? No problem." Andy grinned.

I grinned back. Then my smile drooped.

"What is it this time?" asked Andy.

"It's just . . . well, where am I going to get a one-boy band to play for Tessa's teacher?"

"That's the simplest problem yet. You'll borrow mine."

"Oh, Andy, I—"

"Yes, you can," he cut me off. "There's one thing, though. We'll have to call it a one-*girl* band."

"Oh, Andy, you're the best friend . . ." I started to say. Then I stopped and thought about Tessa, the person I was doing all this for. I looked at Andy again. "The second-best friend," I said with a grin.

21

"Can't you even give me a hint?" Tessa asked.

I shook my head. "You'll see as soon as Ms. Gerard gets here. But I can tell you one thing: It's not a harp." I giggled.

Tessa giggled, too, even though she didn't know the whole joke. "Or a piano," she said.

"No . . . it's definitely not . . . a piano," I said, still giggling.

"You're impossible, Lizzie Silver. I have a mind to go right down to the garage and see just what it is."

"You do and I'll be so mad at you I won't go to Hair Today with you tomorrow."

"You promised," said Tessa. If there's anything she hates, it's getting her hair cut. She always makes me go with her—not that I mind.

"So did you. No peeking until Ms. Gerard gets here."

Tessa sighed. "Okay. But you didn't even thank me for taking care of Markham's animals for two extra days."

"For which you made an extra six dollars," I pointed out. "But thanks anyway. How's Lavinia?"

"Cooing like crazy."

"Oh, good."

After a pause, she said, "I'm sorry Robin was such a jerk."

"Well, I was kind of jerky myself. . . . You know what I got in the mail today?"

"What?"

"An autographed picture of him. It said, 'To Elizabeth Silver, my favorite Merry Man. Yours, Byron Lord.' "

"Oh, no."

"Oh, yes."

"He must've sent it before the weekend and the mail was slow."

"No, it was postmarked on Monday."

"I guess he has a short memory."

I nodded.

"But anyway, I'm glad that kid Andy turned out to be nice."

"Yeah," I said. I didn't tell her how nice. I was keeping the one-girl band a secret until the last minute. I was feeling pretty confident, though. I'd played it for

Andy and his mother and they'd said it was great. And when I came back home, I played it for my family. "What do you think?" I asked them.

"Different," said my mother.

"Clever," said my dad.

"Dumb," said Rona, but she doesn't count.

I didn't tell them why I was playing it. I could tell my mom still didn't understand why I hadn't stuck with the harp instead. But I didn't tell her I never would be able to play "When the Saints Go Marching In" on it by now—even with a nicer teacher than Mr. Jasper.

Tessa and I heard a car pull up into the driveway. Neither of her parents were home, so she and I went down to open the door.

Ms. Gerard is a plump woman with a friendly smile. I've met her a couple of times and she's always been nice to me. This time was no exception.

"Hello, Lizzie," she said. "Tessa tells me you're going to give us a bit of a concert today."

I nodded. "I guess you could call it that."

"Tessa also said the instrument is to be a surprise."

I nodded again.

"Good. I love surprises."

She and Tessa went into the "music room," which is the room with Tessa's piano in it. I went into the garage.

I took the sheet off the one-girl band. I had brought

169

it to Tessa's in the little red wagon I haven't used since I was a little kid. First I took out the cymbals and strapped them to my knees. Then I slipped the strap of the autoharp over my shoulder. I put the kazoo rack (the metal contraption) around my neck and carried the drum, standing cymbals and tambourine in my hands. "Ah, but a girl's reach should exceed her grasp, Or what's a heaven for?" I murmured.

"Close your eyes," I called out. "Okay?"

"Okay," answered Tessa and Ms. Gerard.

I walked into the music room, trying not to crash the cymbals or rattle the tambourine. Tessa and Ms. Gerard were seated on a loveseat. I set the drum, standing cymbals, and tambourine in place. "When I count to three, you can open your eyes," I said. "One . . . two . . ." I took a deep breath. "Three!"

Tessa and Ms. Gerard opened their eyes. When she saw my band, Tessa's eyes widened in amazement. Ms. Gerard's didn't widen. They twinkled.

I plunged right into my number. By the time I got to the second verse—where I added the cymbals—Ms. Gerard was clapping along.

I had an inspiration. I stopped playing the kazoo and yelled, "Everybody sing—'Oh when the saints . . . go marching in . . . Oh when the saints go marching in . . . You know I want to be in that number . . . When the saints go marching in.' "

Ms. Gerard and Tessa sang along.

170

Then I did my big finish, the way Andy taught me. I flipped the tambourine up into my hand, shook it and held the last note on the kazoo an extra long time.

I bowed as well as I could with the autoharp in the way.

Ms. Gerard and Tessa clapped like crazy.

"Wonderful!" Ms. Gerard said. "That was just wonderful! I haven't heard a one-girl band in years."

I felt my chest puff up. Andy says there's nothing like applause to make you feel good. Now I know what he means.

"You were terrific, Lizzie. Where'd you learn to play that?" asked Tessa.

"Andy Frobish taught me. It's his band."

"Wonderful," said Ms. Gerard again. "He must be talented, too."

I turned to her eagerly. "Does that mean you think I'm talented?"

"Most definitely. You have a good sense of rhythm and a delightful enthusiasm."

"Oh, wow! I've got talent! Did you hear that, Tessa? I've got musical talent after all."

Both Tessa and Ms. Gerard smiled at me.

"So how long before I can get into Pemborough?" I asked.

Ms. Gerard's smile changed to a puzzled look. "I don't understand what you mean."

"You know, Pemborough. The school Tessa's going

to. I made a bet with her that if you said I had enough talent to get in there—with some work, of course— she'd wait to go till next year. But if you think I'm good enough now, maybe I can get in sooner."

Ms. Gerard smiled again, but this time it was a different smile. It was the kind of smile somebody gives you when she's feeling sorry for you. "Tessa didn't explain the reason for your concert, Lizzie," she said.

"She didn't?"

"No."

"Would you like a cup of tea, Ms. Gerard?" Tessa asked suddenly.

"Yes. I'd love one," she answered.

Tessa left the room quickly.

"Lizzie, have a seat," said Ms. Gerard.

I took off my kazoo rack, autoharp and cymbals and sat across from her on the piano bench.

"When I was about your age," she said, "I had a really good friend named Margie. We did everything together—we even both ran away from home together once when we were six. Then, one day, she told me her family was going to move to another state two hundred miles away. I tried to get her parents to let her live with me and my family, but they just laughed at me. I suggested she and I run away again together, but she said she was too old for that. The week before they were to go, I called up and pretended to be the person whose house they'd bought. I said I'd changed my mind about selling it and they could have their money back. Of course, Margie's father knew it was me all along. Finally, the night before they left, I went over to their house and sneaked into their moving truck. They didn't find me until they were one hundred miles away. They had to turn around and come right back."

"But your friend moved away anyway?" I asked.

"Yes. She moved away."

There was a pause, and then I said, "Ms. Gerard, you don't think I'll get into Pemborough, do you? You don't really think I'm talented after all."

"I really do think you're talented, Lizzie. But you don't have the kind of talent a school like Pemborough is looking for. Tessa does, so Pemborough is the right place for her. Your place is somewhere else. Somewhere just as special, but different."

I felt my eyes fill up and my lips tremble. I bit them.

"I don't think I want that tea after all," Ms. Gerard said, standing up. She walked to the doorway. Then she turned, looked at me and said, "You're a remarkable person, Lizzie Silver. I hope Tessa appreciates you."

"I do appreciate her," Tessa said, appearing in the doorway.

"Why don't we skip your piano lesson today, Tessa? I'll let myself out," said Ms. Gerard, and she left.

Tessa set down the cup and saucer she was carrying.

"Oh, Tessa," I whispered. "Who's going to feed Ariadne when I go on vacation?"

Tessa's eyes filled up, too. "Who's going to go with me to get my hair cut?" she said.

Without another word, we threw our arms around each other and cried until we couldn't cry anymore.

22

"Sometimes the clouds need a washing,
Sometimes the blue is too cold,
Sometimes the sun's only joshing,
Sometimes the moon looks so old.

"Sometimes a rainbow surprises,
Sometimes the fog looks like lace,
Sometimes the stars wear disguises,
Sometimes it rains on my face.

"But only in July . . ."

Buster paused, looked at the crowd, and said the last
line with a flourish:

"Have I seen a mustard sky."

Instead of applauding, we all bounced the bright balloons we'd been given as soon as we entered the little grove in the park Buster had chosen for the Poem-In.

There wasn't a big crowd—maybe forty people or so. But a lot of them had brought poems to read, and everyone was having a good time. Buster's family and friends were there, including Tessa and her parents, Grandma and Grandpa Brown, and Markham the Magnificent. Surprisingly enough, my whole family was there, too ("Why not?" said my dad. "I haven't been to any kind of an 'in' in a long time.")—even Rona.

Toby Glickstein was not there. It seems that Rona had sprinkled their conversations with so much information about Robin Hood that Toby told her he was tired of playing second fiddle to a legend. I thought Rona was going to be mad at me for helping her get so full of all that information, but instead, she actually seemed to find it funny. And besides, she now had her eye on this big guy named Frank Stein. I don't think he's much next to Toby. I mean, Toby, at least, is smart. When I asked Frank Stein if his middle initial was "N," he just looked at me blankly and said, "Huh?"

The big surprise of the Poem-In was that Andy came. Buster was right. Andy does live near me. I'm really glad about that. It will be hard not having Tessa around, and Andy's being here will help, I think.

Andy even brought a poem to read. When he got

up to read it, Tessa nudged me. "I'm glad you made friends with him. He's cute. I like his red hair."

I gave her a look. "Tessa, I don't want you to go to Pemborough. I tried my best to stop you. But you're going. And I'm going to miss you a lot. However, if you start going dumb-dumb over boys, not only will I *not* miss you—I'll be glad you've gone!"

Tessa swatted me. I swatted her back.

Andy's poem was short and funny:

"When I was walking on the ocean floor,
There were so many sights to adore.
But one sight gave me a fright:
It was a whale with a big long tail
And a belly fat.
And I went so close
That with its tail it went
Spat, spat, spat.

Written by Andrew Frobish, age six," he finished.

We all laughed. When he came back to where we were sitting, he said, "How'd you like my poem, Lizzie?"

"Oh, I *loved* it," I said in an exaggerated voice.

Andy laughed. But my mom said, "Lizzie, it's so nice to see you interested in poetry. Don't you think so, David?"

"Personally, I prefer spiders or Robin Hood," my dad answered.

"Well, I don't," said my mother. "I'm glad Lizzie's

over her Robin Hood phase. It was so . . . limiting. In fact, I hope Lizzie's past obsessions in general . . ."

I caught Rona mouthing Mom's words along with her. Usually that would've made me laugh. But I was thinking about what Mom had said. It seemed to me I *was* past obsessions. I still liked spiders and Robin Hood (in his books), but in a different way from how I had liked them before. I wondered if that meant I was growing up.

I was still thinking about that when Buster said it was time for the grand finale. Andy and the other people who had brought poems to read folded them up and tied them to the balloons' strings.

"Okay. Everybody ready?" said Buster.

A silence fell over the crowd.

"This is kind of neat," Tessa whispered.

I looked at her and smiled. It was about time she said something nice about Buster—even if it wasn't exactly about him.

"Okay," he said. "On the count of three, you know what to do. One . . . two . . ." He paused. "Three!" he shouted.

With a cheer, we all let go of our balloons. They floated up, up, up with their poem passengers. Soon the sky was red, green, blue, yellow, pink, white, purple and orange with them. Everyone kept cheering.

"That's a truly poetic finale—don't you think so, Lizzie?" my mom said.

"Yes," I said.

179

"Don't tell me Lizzie's given up science for poetry," Dad said.

"This is poetic, but it's also scientific," I said. "You see, those balloons have helium in them. Helium is lighter than air. That's why those balloons float right up. But what I wonder is how somebody discovered it and . . ."

"Spare us," said Rona.

"I didn't know you were interested in science," said Andy.

"Oh, boy," said Tessa. "Andy's got a lot to learn about you, Lizzie."

"I like science, too," said Andy. "In fact, if I weren't planning to be an actor when I grow up, I'd be an astronaut, exploring new worlds, boldly going where no man—or woman—has gone before."

"An astronaut!" I said. "Wow! I never thought of being that. An astronaut." My eyes lit up.

"Uh-oh," said Rona.

"What kind of training do astronauts need? When do they start? How old do you have to be?"

"Lizzie," Tessa warned me, laughing.

"Do you think they'll ever put kids in space?"

"Here we go again." Mom sighed.

Dad laughed.

I ignored them both. I could see myself in a silver space suit and helmet, sitting behind the controls of a spaceship.

"Approaching an ion storm. Hold steady," I said.

"Yes, Captain Silver," answered the helmsman.

Captain Silver. I smiled proudly. Captain Silver, also known, by friends and foes alike, as Elizabeth Silver of Planet Earth.